Lucky Lady

Lucky Lady

SUSAN SAUNDERS

HarperCollins*Publishers*

Lucky Lady
Copyright © 2000 by Susan Saunders

For information address HarperCollins Children's Books, a division of
HarperCollins Publishers, 1350 Avenue of the Americas, New York, NY 10019.
www.harperchildrens.com

Library of Congress Cataloging-in-Publication Data
Saunders, Susan.
  Lucky Lady / Susan Saunders.
      p.   cm.
  Summary: On a summer visit to her grandfather's ranch in Texas, twelve-year-old
Jamie impulsively spends all her money on a wild filly and tries to figure out how
to train her.
  ISBN 0-380-97784-2 (hc. : alk. paper)
  [1. Horses—Fiction.   2. Ranch life—Texas—Fiction.   3. Texas—Fiction.
4. Grandfathers—Fiction.]   I. Title.
PZ7.S197884Lu 2000   99-42648
[Fic]—dc21   CIP
                                                                            AC

                  10   9   8   7   6   5   4
                              ❖
                       First Edition

For my father

Lucky Lady

1

THE PLANE TOUCHED DOWN, BOUNCING ONCE, twice, as its wheels met the runway.

Jamie Cooper pressed her forehead against the window, squinting into the glaring sunlight outside. Several brown-and-white cows and calves grazed calmly on the far side of a wire fence.

In just a few minutes, Jamie would see her grandfather for the first time in four years. Would they recognize each other?

She'd grown a foot, at least. And her granddad had to look older—he was seventy-three now.

"Seventy-three or not, I won't let him dump on Mom," she promised herself, frowning.

Not that he was likely to, not in so many words, anyway—he'd never been much of a talker. But he and Jamie's mom had had even less to say to each other since he'd stayed with them in Maine, right after Jamie's father died.

"Now there's no reason for you not to move back home," he'd said.

"This *is* home," Jamie's mom had told him, and that was that.

As she'd explained to Jamie, "Dad always thought I'd go to junior college in south Texas, marry a rancher, and live there for the rest of my life. He was so shocked when I got a scholarship to an Eastern university that he didn't think to say no to me, and he's still trying to correct his mistake."

Maybe it was easier if they didn't see each other very often. Anyway, Jamie's granddad hadn't visited again, and he rarely called her mother. He hadn't really kept up with Jamie, either, aside from Christmas and birthday cards with a twenty-dollar bill inside. Which wasn't right, because the bad feelings had nothing to do with her.

Then, a few weeks ago, Jamie's mom had gotten a big writing job for a travel magazine. She'd be away, in southeast Asia, for two months. She said she'd feel easier if she knew Jamie was staying with family while she was gone. "Dad's all the family we've got now—and you two should get better acquainted, anyway."

When she noticed the expression on Jamie's face she added, "You'll have a lot of fun, riding around the ranch."

So here she was, whether she wanted to be or not. The plane braked to a stop with a jerk, and Jamie glanced out the window again. She and her parents had flown down for a half dozen summer vacations before her dad's first heart attack. The Santa Rosa terminal looked pretty much the same: a low, stucco rectangle with a few dusty palm trees leaning into it.

A small crowd of people had gathered at the edge of the building to meet the plane: kids in baseball caps, women in shorts, two or three men wearing Western shirts. But Jamie didn't see her grandfather.

She stood up and pulled her backpack out of the overhead rack. The door of the plane popped open, and the cabin filled with steamy July air, salty smelling like the Gulf of Mexico.

Jamie waited for the dozen or so other passengers to clear out before she made her way up the aisle.

She nodded when the stewardess asked, "Do you have someone meeting you?" Then she stepped through the doorway and paused at the top of the stairs.

Shimmering eddies of heat rose from the tarmac below her. The small crowd of greeters was hurrying into the air-conditioned terminal, along with the passengers they'd met.

But Jamie's grandfather was nowhere in sight.

Did he forget I was coming? Jamie wondered, suddenly worried.

She started down the stairs, digging into her waist pack for change for a phone call. But she knew her granddad hardly ever bothered to answer his phone, and her mom was already in Bangkok or someplace. There was nobody she could call.

For a moment, her fingers closed on the roll of bills her mother had given her "for expenses."

"Two hundred dollars should get you through the summer, with plenty left over," Mom had said. It was the most money Jamie had ever seen at one time.

That's when the thought came to her out of nowhere: *I'll bet that two hundred dollars would buy me a bus ticket back to Maine! I could stay with Laurie until Mom gets home. Or at Sara's house, and help out at their shop. If he's not waiting . . .*

Before Jamie reached the sliding-glass doors of the terminal, she was thinking: *Why don't I leave a message at the information desk, take a cab into Santa Rosa, and find the Greyhound bus station? I don't want to be here, and he doesn't want me, either.* She looked around for the baggage claim.

Then she heard a loud laugh and turned to see two men in straw cowboy hats standing near the lockers against the far wall, deep in conversation.

Jamie didn't know the big red-faced guy, but the man with his back to the room had silvery hair, he wore his hat slightly cocked to one side, and he looked familiar. She walked closer, until she could read the cream-colored letters on the man's Western belt: CAMERON.

"That is Granddad," Jamie murmured, just briefly considering following her plan and sneaking away before he saw her. Instead, she found she was too angry. He cared so little about seeing her that he couldn't be bothered to meet her at the plane, not even after four years. He wasn't going to get away with it!

Jamie marched over to the men and glared straight at her grandfather.

The tall guy was so deep into a story about a horse he'd once owned that he didn't notice Jamie at first. Then his gaze slid over to her. "Can we help you, honey?"

And finally Jamie's grandfather glanced at her, too. When his expression didn't change, she said, "I'm Jamie Cooper."

"Jamie?" he repeated, as though he couldn't quite connect this Jamie with the one he'd seen four years earlier. He had changed, too—he looked shorter and thinner and grayer than she remembered.

"This is Carolyn's girl?" the large man exclaimed. "Pleased to meet you, Jamie." He shook her hand. "I'm Joe Stacy. I knew your mama when she was—"

"I didn't recognize you," Jamie's granddad said.

He wasn't much for hugging—Grandmama had been the one who'd hugged and kissed everybody. But he rested his hands lightly on Jamie's shoulders. "You're practically grown."

"I'm almost thirteen," Jamie reminded him firmly.

Her grandfather seemed tired, and his blue eyes were kind of sad.

"You have Carolyn's blond hair." Mr. Stacy was smiling down at her.

Walt Cameron suddenly cleared his throat loudly. "We better find your suitcase and head on down the road."

"That's right. She's bound to be worn out, flying so far . . . Where is Carolyn living now, Walt?" Mr. Stacy said.

"Covington, Maine," Jamie answered.

"Maine sure is a long way from home," said Mr. Stacy, shaking his head.

"Maine *is* home," Jamie said, catching her grandfather's eye, so that he'd know exactly where she stood on the issue.

Mr. Stacy went on, "Well, good to see you, Walt. And you too, Jamie—you have a nice stay here in south Texas."

"See you later, Joe," said Jamie's granddad over his shoulder as he headed toward the baggage claim. He was limping, as if one of his old riding injuries had finally caught up with him.

It was a two-hour drive from the airport to Wilcox, and it would take another ten minutes or so to get to her granddad's ranch. Jamie climbed into the passenger side of Walt Cameron's air-conditioned truck, determined not to say a word.

But her granddad didn't say anything, either, not until he'd maneuvered the truck through five o'clock traffic in Santa Rosa and turned onto Farm Road 126 at the edge of town. Then his shoulders slumped a little. "I'm not used to all these cars."

Jamie shrugged, thinking of the world-class rush hours in Portland or Boston. Her grandfather glanced sideways at her before turning his attention to the road again. It stretched out flat and straight under a cloudless, electric-blue sky. Barbed wire fences on both sides of it enclosed pastures dotted with rangy cattle.

Large stands of prickly pear cactus and lone mesquites were the only greens in a red-brown landscape. Here and there, the earth had actually cracked open under the scorching summer sun.

"Wow, it's really dry," Jamie murmured in spite of herself.

"Hasn't rained more than an inch in seven months," her grandfather said. "A man in Wilcox started a brush fire just by driving across the prairie—heat from his exhaust pipe sparked the grass."

"Is there enough for your cattle to eat?"

"No cattle to worry about—I got rid of 'em when I leased the ranch for grazing," Mr. Cameron replied shortly.

Jamie turned to stare at him.

Whenever she'd visited before, he'd been busy mending fences, fixing windmills, taking care of his own cattle, or helping out neighboring ranchers. If he'd leased his land, what did he do with himself?

"I know your mother'll sell everything the minute I'm gone, anyway," Mr. Cameron added grimly, sounding as though he might be going soon.

Jamie studied him out of the corner of her eye. His skin was leathery and wrinkled from all the years he'd spent in the sun, and his hair had faded from gray to white in places. But his hands were steady on the steering wheel, and he didn't even have to wear glasses. Granddad wasn't *that* old.

"What about the horses?" she asked after a while.

She'd been taking riding lessons for the last three years, and she'd been looking forward to riding around the ranch on her own.

"Trompas died of old age. I sold Dandy to a neighbor for his grandkids, and the others went, too," Mr. Cameron said. "No cattle to work, so I didn't need a bunch of horses hanging around, making nuisances of themselves."

"Even Samson?" Samson had always been her grandfather's favorite, a big sorrel born on the ranch who'd become the best cowhorse in the county.

"No, he's still there." Mr. Cameron added, "Nobody would want him—he's as old and worn out as I am."

No cattle, no horses . . . as far as Jamie could tell, she'd be spending two months in the middle of nowhere with absolutely nothing to do and a granddad who'd decided that his life was practically over.

2

*B*EFORE THEY'D MADE IT HALFWAY TO WILCOX, Jamie fell sound asleep in her granddad's truck. When her eyes flew open the next morning, she barely remembered stumbling up the sidewalk to the ranch house and through the dark kitchen, to fall into bed in the spare room.

She wasn't sure what had awakened her. Then she heard it again: the sharp, mournful whinny of a horse. Was Samson calling to his missing friends?

Jamie glanced around the room that had been her mother's. On the walls there were glass cases lined with blue ribbons that Jamie's mom had won riding in quarter horse shows. Her gold and silver trophies crowned the bookcase, several from the summer before she left for college and never came back.

When Jamie looked at her watch and subtracted for time changes—it was 7:35—she realized she hadn't eaten for almost twenty-four hours. Suddenly she was starving!

She slipped into her jeans and shirt from the day before, laced up her sneakers, pulled her hair back into a short ponytail, and started down the hall. She glanced into her grandfather's room on her way past. His bed looked lumpy under a faded quilt. On the wall above the headboard, there was a big black-and-white photograph of him and Grandmama when they were young, wearing high-crowned felt hats and string ties. They had big smiles on their faces. Her grandfather hadn't smiled once since she'd arrived.

She sort of expected to find him in the kitchen, making breakfast. But the kitchen was empty.

Jamie crossed the tile floor to peer through the screen door. She spotted her granddad standing in the corral beyond the barn and windmill. The large, caramel-colored animal beside him was old Samson, munching on his morning oats.

Jamie's stomach growled. "I'm ready for some oats myself," she mumbled.

And maybe that's all she'd get. When she looked into the refrigerator, she found a quart of milk, three cans of Coke, and a jar of jalapeño peppers.

Maybe there was something to eat in the pine wall cabinets. She flicked the light switch beside the screen door, glancing up at the ceiling when nothing happened. A couple of wires hung out of the round hole where a fixture used to be.

Jamie noticed an old water stain in the far corner of the room and curls of paint peeling away from the walls. She sank down onto one of the wooden chairs beside the small table and listened to her stomach growl. From the looks of things, her grandfather wasn't up to doing much fixing. Or eating.

Then the screen door creaked open. Her granddad winced as he swung his leg over the threshold and stepped into the kitchen.

"Good morning. The light's not working," Jamie said.

"Um-hmm. I didn't know what you'd want for breakfast, so I got some cereal . . ."

He lifted three boxes down from the top shelf of the cabinet closest to the sink. "Sugar Pops. Cheerios. Froot Loops."

"Cheerios," Jamie said, taking the box from him. "Thanks."

Her granddad edged past her into the living room, as she opened the refrigerator for milk. What *did* he eat?

Her grandmother had served huge meals: platters of fried chicken or a big roast, hot rolls or biscuits, two or three vegetables, fruit pies for dessert. And pancakes and sausages for breakfast—Jamie could almost taste them.

She sat at the kitchen table and ate her cereal, listening to her grandfather on the phone in the living room. "Yeah, if you could . . . appreciate it . . . the trip was just fine . . . Thanks, Gilbert."

When he walked back into the kitchen he announced, "The electrician's coming this morning."

He snacked on a couple of fistfuls of Sugar Pops straight from the box before he pushed open the screen door. "I'll be out in the barn."

Jamie was getting the idea that she'd be on her own a lot of the time.

She finished her cereal and rinsed the bowl in the sink. Then she poured some Sugar Pops into her hand for Samson.

The old sorrel horse nickered eagerly when he saw her heading toward the corral. "At least somebody's glad to see me." As she walked through the east gate, he stretched his neck out and sniffed her hair. Then he nibbled the sweetened cereal from Jamie's hand, his soft nose ticking her palm.

"You're looking good, Samson."

She patted his strong chest. Jamie had seen her granddad ride this horse to rope a stampeding bull. Samson had stopped the huge animal dead in its tracks as easily as if it were a baby calf. But Samson's cowpunching days were over. His caramel coat was speckled with white hairs now, and he had a hard lump the size of Jamie's fist above one knee.

"You'd like to be brushed, wouldn't you, boy?" she asked, pulling a twig out of his mane. "Just let me find a currycomb."

The tack room was in the barn. Jamie could hear her granddad puttering around in his workshop at the other end of the low wooden building, his staticky radio tuned to a country-and-western station.

At least he hadn't sold his best roping saddle. Jamie ran her fingers across the hand-tooled flowers on its cantle. Her mom's trophy saddle rested on a rack, too, its silver conchos gleaming in the half light.

Jamie chose a currycomb and a dandy brush from a box on the floor and stepped outside again. She'd brushed Samson's neck and back and was starting on his left side when a faded gray Jeep came bumping down the road. It screeched to a stop near the house, stirring up a cloud of dust, and a black-haired man jumped out of it. He had a friendly smile under his droopy mustache.

"You have to be Jamie!" the man said, striding over to the corral. "I'm Gilbert Ochoa." They shook hands. "And that's my boy Arnoldo."

The kid climbing out of the Jeep muffled a yawn, as though he'd been pulled from his bed before he was ready to wake up.

Arnoldo Ochoa had thick black hair like his dad's, but his was shorter and spikier. He was wearing baggy jeans, a red

T-shirt, a navy-and-white Dallas Cowboys cap, and dark glasses.

"Hey," Arnoldo said when he was close enough.

He was taller than Jamie and twice as broad.

"Hey."

"I've got some wiring to fix," Mr. Ochoa told them. "How about you two getting acquainted?"

As his father headed for the house with a toolbox, Arnoldo plopped down on an overturned feed bucket. He pushed his dark glasses back on his head and rubbed his eyes. "So where're you from?"

"I was born in Boston. But we live in Maine now." Jamie noticed he had a tiny silver stud in his right ear.

"I've never been out of state, except to Mexico, and that's only thirty miles from here," Arnoldo said. "What's it like in Maine?"

"Lots of rocks. And evergreens. And water. Our house isn't far from the Atlantic Ocean."

"Does it snow where you live?"

"Uh-huh, for months at a time."

"It snowed once in Wilcox, thirteen years ago. But I missed it," Arnoldo said. "It was right before I was born."

So he was her age, more or less.

He shifted gears. "What'll you do out here in the sticks all summer long?" He waved his hand at the mesquites and cactus patches.

"I don't have a clue," Jamie admitted. "I thought I'd be riding at least, but my granddad sold all of his horses. Except Samson."

She pointed to the sorrel horse dozing on the far side of the corral fence. "And he's too old to bother."

"Your granddad's a pretty old guy, too—my dad thinks he's slipping."

Jamie had been thinking so herself, but hearing someone else say it out loud jolted her.

Arnoldo pulled his shades back down over his eyes and stared into space for a minute. Then he said, "We've got an extra bike at our house. It's my older brother's, but he's in the army. You could use it to ride back and forth to town. I could show you all-l-l the sights in Wilcox." He grinned at her.

"That would be cool," Jamie said, hoping he meant it.

"I'll tell my dad to bring the bike out here first thing tomorrow."

Mr. Ochoa finished rewiring the kitchen light in ten minutes flat, and was ready to leave for his next job.

"Mrs. Campbell down the highway blew all of her fuses last night, and I need to figure out why." He dropped the heavy toolbox into the back of the Jeep with a thud.

"Catch you tomorrow, Jamie," Arnoldo said.

She was waving good-bye when her grandfather rumbled through the screen door, "Telephone. It's your mother."

Jamie raced past him, across the kitchen, and into the

living room. She grabbed the phone off the end table and practically shouted, "Mom?"

"Hi, sweetie. How was your trip?" Her mom's voice sounded so clear that for a split second Jamie thought, *Maybe she decided not to go!*

"Where are you, Mom?"

"I'm in Hong Kong. How's Dad doing? He could barely manage a 'hello.'"

"Just a second," Jamie said in a low voice.

She put the phone down and peered into the kitchen. Sure enough, her grandfather had left the house.

"He's outside now," Jamie said when she picked up the phone again. "Mom, he got rid of everything."

"What do you mean?"

"He leased the ranch and sold his cattle . . . and all of the horses except Samson, who's in bad shape."

There was silence on her mother's end of the line.

"Mom?"

"I'm here."

"Mr. Ochoa says he's definitely slipping."

"Who's Mr. Ochoa?"

"The electrician."

Actually, it seemed to Jamie that her granddad was doing more than "slipping." Sliding, maybe, toward the end of his life.

"I had no idea," her mom was saying. "I'd imagined you

riding around the ranch with him, helping with the cattle . . . I'm really sorry, Jamie. I'd better hang up, or I'll miss my plane to Saigon," she added. "I'll be in Vietnam for two weeks. There probably aren't many phones in the Mekong Delta, but I'll call as often as I can."

"Okay, Mom," Jamie said, missing her painfully.

"Your granddad's alone too much. Think of things you can do together." Her voice was fading.

"I'll try."

"Talk to you soon. Bye." Her mom was gone.

Jamie hung up the phone and walked slowly outside.

Her grandfather was sitting on a stump at the corner of the house, whittling a stick with his pocketknife. He didn't bother to look up.

"Mom's on her way to Saigon," Jamie said loudly.

"Texas never was good enough for Carolyn," her grandfather muttered. He tossed the stick aside, folded his pocketknife, and stood up. "I have to drive into town to gas up the truck and buy some rolled oats for Samson—his teeth are worn out. You'd better come along."

3

$\mathcal{I}$T WAS A SILENT TRIP INTO WILCOX, WITH JAMIE missing her mom, and Walt Cameron glaring through the windshield as though he had plenty on his mind, too. They stopped at Sam's Service Station on Main Street to fill up the truck, then at Montalvo's Feed Store for three bags of rolled oats for Samson. But before Mr. Cameron could start the drive back to the ranch, Jamie said, "Where is the supermarket?"

"What do you need?" Her grandfather slowed down for the yellow light.

"Something to cook." She couldn't live on cereal for the next two months.

"The oven doesn't work, so I usually eat here in town," her grandfather said.

"I can cook on top of the stove." She helped her mom with meals all the time. And the whole seventh grade at her school had had cooking classes last semester.

Her granddad made a sharp left turn and pulled into the parking lot at the Wilcox Food Fair.

For lunch, Jamie chose sliced turkey, a loaf of bread, and some tomatoes. She picked out chopped meat, salad greens, and frozen corn for dinner, and muffins and eggs for breakfast. Her grandfather paid without a word.

They were on their way out of town with the groceries when Jamie noticed a sprawling green building at the end of a wide gravel road. "What's that?"

"Auction barn. There's a cattle auction every Thursday."

"Tomorrow's Thursday." Mom wanted them to do stuff together, right? And Jamie had never seen a cattle auction.

"I'm not in the cattle business anymore."

Fine. So maybe Arnoldo and I can go, Jamie thought. If he remembered about the bike.

Arnoldo Ochoa was a kid of his word—he showed up at the ranch house the next morning at nine o'clock sharp.

Jamie was in her room, writing a note to her friend Sara,

while her granddad watched The Weather Channel on TV. She jumped to her feet and raced for the kitchen door when she heard a car horn.

The gray Jeep was already parked at the side of the house. Arnoldo and his dad were lifting a silver fifteen-speed out of the back.

"We pumped up the tires," Arnoldo said, rolling the bike toward Jamie.

"And oiled the gears," said his dad. "It's in good shape, just a little rusty."

"You're sure it's okay for me to borrow it?" Jamie said, taking hold of the handlebars.

"Junior's driving a tank now," said Mr. Ochoa. "He'll be glad somebody's riding his bike."

"Morning, Gilbert. What are you doing here?" Mr. Cameron had come to the kitchen door.

"We brought Jamie some wheels so she can tool around Wilcox when she wants to."

"That's mighty nice of you." He sounded a little surprised by Mr. Ochoa's thoughtfulness.

"Want to go into town right now?" Arnoldo said to Jamie. "I've got my bike, too." He pointed to a black mountain bike still lying in the back of the Jeep.

"Sure!" Jamie said. "Okay?"

Her grandfather nodded.

"We'll have lunch at Concha's Fajitas," Arnoldo told Jamie.

"Great!" Jamie said, hopping onto Gilbert Jr.'s bike.

"See you guys," Mr. Ochoa said.

"We'll stop by my house later. I want to show you Chester—that's our new dog," Arnoldo told Jamie.

"What about your new little brother?" his dad said, laughing when Arnoldo rolled his eyes.

Jamie and Arnoldo took off, riding down the deep ruts in the dirt road to the highway. By the time they turned onto the blacktop, Jamie was sweaty.

"It must be a hundred degrees out here!" She wiped her face with her hand.

"It's early yet," Arnoldo replied. "One afternoon last week, the thermometer on our patio went up to one-thirteen."

It was seven boiling miles to Wilcox. Superheated air swirled around them as eighteen-wheelers rattled past, filled with bellowing cattle. When they reached the road sign at the outskirts of town—WILCOX: POPULATION 2132—Jamie could see the huge trucks joining a line of smaller trucks and cars, all rolling toward the auction barn.

"Hey, what about checking out the auction?" she said as they coasted around a curve.

"Five hundred cows in a row?" Arnoldo said. "Bo-o-oring."

"I've never been to one. We wouldn't have to stay long."

"Well . . . okay. It gets going at ten, and the beginning's the best, anyway, because they have pigs and goats and sometimes even a few horses before they start in with the cows. Besides, the lobby's air-conditioned, and there's a soda fountain. We can grab some drinks and cool off."

They turned onto the gravel road and pedaled along the shoulder, past bumper-to-bumper trucks and cars headed for the parking lot.

"No bike locks?" Jamie asked as they leaned their bikes against the side of the green stucco building.

"These cowboys probably don't want to steal our bikes. You think?" Arnoldo raised his eyebrows at her and grinned.

They climbed the steps, pushed open a set of swinging doors, and walked through them.

The air-conditioning in the lobby hit Jamie's damp face and back like an Arctic wind. Arnoldo was edging through a crowd of men in straw hats and Western boots, all of them talking and laughing while they waited for the auction to start.

He waved at a plump, middle-aged woman behind a desk in the glass-fronted office, and she smiled and waved back. "That's my cousin Irma." Then he led Jamie into the coffee shop.

They ordered two fountain Cokes from the teenage girl behind the counter.

"Jamie, this is Annabelle," Arnoldo said when she brought them their drinks. "Annabelle's the captain of the Wilcox Badgerettes basketball team."

"Hey, Jamie."

"Hi, Annabelle."

Jamie dug into her waist pack, and Annabelle and Arnoldo both stared at the thick roll of bills she pulled out of it.

"Wow!" Arnoldo said, impressed. "You're rich!"

"Oh. No, this is supposed to last me for the whole summer," Jamie explained, embarrassed. She peeled off a five-dollar bill to pay for both Cokes, and stuffed the change into her pack.

Then she and Arnoldo crossed the lobby and walked through the door leading to the auction ring itself. Half of the open space beyond it was filled with floor-to-ceiling concrete bleachers. The bleachers were jammed with cattle buyers and sellers, facing a semicircular pen fenced with thick steel pipes.

Once Arnoldo and Jamie had squeezed into an empty spot near the top of the bleachers, he said, "That pen's called the ring. The animals run into it through the iron gate on the right, and out through the one on the left."

He went on, "The auctioneer starts things off by setting a price. And then anyone here in the bleachers can hold up his hand to bid a higher price. Highest bidder takes home the animal."

He pointed to a platform above and behind the ring. "That's where the auctioneer stands . . . and there he is—Mr. Mike McBride."

Jamie saw a balding man with wire glasses stepping up to a microphone.

"Morning, folks," Mr. McBride said to the audience. "Let's get this show on the road!"

A young guy opened the gate at the right, and a white goat with long, droopy ears bolted into the ring.

"A fine Anglo-Nubian doe—you don't see many of these down here. We'll start the bidding at eighty dollars," Mr. McBride said. "Do I see eighty dollars?"

He began his auctioneer's patter, which sounded like "ibidy-ibidy" to Jamie. She was barely able to make out the amounts being bid.

"Ibidy-ibidy-ebidy-eighty . . . gimme-eighty . . . "

"Like Porky Pig cartoons, right?" Arnoldo joked.

Two rows below them, a man wearing a white cowboy hat raised his hand.

"Eighty," Mr. McBride said. "Do I see eighty-five? Ibidy-ibidy-ibidy-eighty-five, eighty-five . . . I see eighty-five," he added when another man bid. "Ninety . . . nibidy-nibidy and ninety from Tony Salinas."

The big white goat sold for one hundred ten dollars. Two more goats ran through the ring, then a huge pinkish-white boar, followed by four smaller pigs.

"He's so cute," Jamie said to Arnoldo, watching a spotted pig trot along the fence.

"Yeah, he's cute, but they're not buying him for a pet."

"They're going to *eat* him!" Jamie realized. "How could they?"

"Sometimes I think about being a vegetarian," said Arnoldo seriously. "Then I ride past Concha's Fajitas . . ."

When the last pig had been sold, the auction ring remained empty for several minutes.

"They'll start running the cattle through now," Arnoldo told Jamie. "And that'll go on all day. Want to get out of here?"

"Sure," Jamie said.

But the iron gate at the right end of the ring flew open with a clang, and it wasn't a cow or a calf that burst through it: It was a horse.

"Wow . . ." Jamie murmured, pausing halfway out of her seat.

Muscles bunched under the horse's skin, which was a rich, creamy yellow. Its mane and tail were black, and so were all four of its legs.

The horse stopped dead in the center of the ring and turned toward the bleachers, its small ears pricked forward, eyes wide open, its nostrils flared. There was a perfect white diamond in the middle of its face.

"Beautiful!" Jamie exclaimed.

"Sit down, young lady, so the rest of us can see that filly," said a man behind Jamie. He went on to tell his neighbor, "From the Anderson Ranch—there's the brand."

The filly had a large rocking *A* on her left shoulder.

"They've raised a lot of winners," the other man said, studying the horse intently.

An interested buzz ran through the bleachers as the auctioneer started the bidding.

"Most of you have figured out this is one of those famous buckskins from the Anderson Ranch," Mr. McBride said into the microphone. "She's a two-year-old, sound and strong, but never rode. I'm goin' to start the bidding at . . . nine hundred dollars, and that's a steal."

The man sitting behind Jamie raised his hand. "I can peddle her later this afternoon for twice that," he said to his friend.

"Nibidy-nibidy-nine-fifty, do-I-see-nine-fifty . . . nine-fifty . . . ," said the auctioneer.

A finger waved at the far side of the bleachers.

"Nine-fifty . . . one thousand," said the auctioneer.

A guy two rows down nodded his head.

The buckskin filly had a broad chest, a short, wide back, and strong hindquarters, traits Jamie knew her riding teacher looked for in a good horse. Her muscles were trembling under her yellow skin.

Mr. McBride pushed the bidding on the filly up to sixteen hundred dollars, and Jamie expected the price to keep rising and rising.

Then, suddenly, everything changed.

The filly might have spooked at a buyer rattling a newspaper in the front row of the bleachers. Or maybe one of the gate men moved too quickly and startled her.

Whatever it was, she snorted loudly and shot backward,

crashing into the pipe fence with her hocks.

She leaned against the fence for a moment, as though she were thinking about how best to save herself. Then she sprang forward and started bucking, taking tremendous leaps, twisting her body in the air, and hitting the ground with all four feet at once.

"Awesome!" said Arnoldo.

The horse whirled and charged straight at the right gate, squealing desperately.

"She's trying to get out!" Jamie said, breathless.

The gate man scrambled out of the way just before the filly rammed her head against the iron gate so hard that it rang.

She fell to her knees, stunned.

The audience groaned.

"You better take a new tack, Mike," a man yelled to the auctioneer.

"You've got a point there, Charlie," the auctioneer said. "Let's start the bidding over at . . . two hundred dollars . . . two hundred . . . two."

"Why's he doing that?" Jamie asked Arnoldo. "Lowering the price so much?"

"That horse is *wild*," Arnoldo said. "Who'd want to pay sixteen hundred dollars for an animal that could hurt you?"

"Two hundred?" Mr. McBride repeated when no one bid.

Jamie glanced around the bleachers. "Come on—somebody

please take her," she murmured. Then she asked Arnoldo, "What if nobody bids?"

"Horsemeat for Europe," he said.

"No way!" Jamie said, her stomach turning.

"Way," said Arnoldo.

The buckskin filly had staggered to her feet again, but her head hung low in defeat. It was heartbreaking.

And almost without thinking, Jamie raised her hand.

"Sold!" the auctioneer said as soon as he spotted it. "To the young lady in the blue shirt for two hundred dollars. What's your name, honey?"

"Jamie." It came out as a croak, so she cleared her throat. "Jamie Cooper."

"Once you've settled your bill at the office," the auctioneer told her, "you can pick up your horse out back, Jamie Cooper."

The filly kicked at the gate men on her way out of the ring.

The guys sitting behind Jamie and Arnoldo were chuckling. "You sure have your work cut out for you," one of them said to Jamie.

"Just getting her home will be a free-for-all," said the other.

"Yeah, Jamie—I can't believe you did this!" Arnoldo said in a low voice.

"Neither can I!"

She was panicking. First, about the money. She'd blown her entire summer fund in a split second, with nothing left over. How was she going to feed the filly, much less buy anything for herself in the next two months?

Second, her granddad. He'd be furious, getting stuck with a wild horse, when he'd gotten rid of tame ones just because he didn't want to be bothered.

Third, the filly. How was Jamie going to get her from the auction barn to the ranch? She couldn't exactly ride her there.

Fourth, even if Jamie managed to get her to the ranch . . . then what? What if the filly was as dangerous as she looked?

Arnoldo stood up and started squeezing past the people in their row.

Jamie stood up, too. Her legs wobbled as she followed Arnoldo down the steps and through the door to the lobby.

"Time to pay up." Arnoldo was staring at her as though she'd totally lost it.

"I know, I know." Jamie dug into her waist pack again, and recalled the Cokes she'd bought earlier.

"Uh . . . could you possibly lend me two dollars and fifty cents, Arnoldo?"

4

JAMIE COUNTED OUT TWO HUNDRED DOLLARS IN tens, fives, ones, and the coins she'd gotten from Arnoldo. She handed all the money over to his cousin Irma in the office, and Irma gave Jamie a receipt for the buckskin filly. Then Jamie and Arnoldo hurried outside.

They climbed up to the narrow catwalk that ran above dozens of square pens under a long tin roof. The pens were crowded with cattle of different colors and sizes, most of them bawling pitifully while they waited to be run through the ring.

"They keep the horses at the very back," Arnoldo yelled to Jamie over the din.

Soon she spotted a patch of creamy yellow—the buckskin filly was alone in a pen. As Jamie and Arnoldo moved closer, she raised her head high to study them suspiciously. Her small, pointed ears were swiveling back and forth, tracking the strange sounds all around her.

"She's amazing," Jamie murmured, gazing into the horse's wide-set, intelligent eyes. "I own this horse," she added, trying to take it in.

"Which is good news for her—she won't be horsemeat. But I don't know about good news for you."

The filly didn't exactly seem grateful—she squealed and stamped her feet. Then she bared her teeth and charged at a white cow and calf in the pen next to hers, skidding to a stop just inches from the fence.

"She is ba-a-ad!" Arnoldo said, half admiringly.

"I can't call my granddad to pick us up. He probably wouldn't come, for one thing," Jamie said. "Plus I don't think he owns a horse trailer anymore."

"Like this horse would strut into a skinny trailer."

Below them, the filly was trying to tear up the fence.

"Hey, I have an idea!" Arnoldo announced. "My uncle Tomas just bought a used ten-ton truck to haul heavy equipment around in—he makes roads and driveways. I'll bet we could walk your horse into the back of it."

"Would your uncle do that?" Jamie said.

"Why not? I'm just about his favorite nephew," Arnoldo said, trotting down the catwalk with Jamie right behind him. "If I can find him . . ."

Arnoldo called his uncle Tomas's cell phone number from the pay phone in the lobby.

"It's ringing," Arnoldo reported to Jamie, "and ringing . . . Hello? . . . Tío! Are you busy? Can you do me a favor?"

Jamie and Arnoldo waited inside the building.

"You don't want to make that horse any jumpier by standing over her on the catwalk," he advised. "Plus it's a lot cooler in here."

They were each finishing their second Coke, on credit from Annabelle, when the doors into the lobby swung open and a dark, stocky guy stepped through them. His navy-blue T-shirt had TOM'S DRIVEWAYS printed across it.

Arnoldo hurried over to give him a hug. "Tío, this is Jamie Cooper. Jamie, my uncle Tomas."

"Hi, Jamie. I understand you have a little transportation problem."

Jamie nodded, and Arnoldo said, "*Major* transportation problem."

"I've got a truck big enough to hold *five* wild horses," Tomas said with a smile. "Let's see what we can do with yours."

He'd pulled his truck up near the steps. The hand-painted navy-blue cab was dented in spots. But the fenced-in truck bed looked solid. Thick wooden planking six feet high enclosed a space around ten square feet.

"Hop in—the other door's stuck." Tomas pulled open the door on the driver's side so Arnoldo and Jamie could slide across the wide seat.

"We'll back up to one of the loading chutes. Then we'll run your horse up the alley, through the chute, and into the truck before she can think about changing her mind—piece of cake."

Jamie's filly had other ideas, though. Even with two of the auction hands helping him, Tomas had a hard time just getting her out of the pen. Each time they aimed her at the open gate, she spun around before she reached it. Ears flattened, she tried to sideswipe the men as she bolted past them into the far corner again.

"Now she's afraid to leave," Jamie said to Arnoldo from their perch on the catwalk. "She doesn't trust them."

"Yeah, why should she trust any humans?"

The three men finally forced the frightened horse out of the pen into a narrow alley leading to the loading chute. One of the guys managed to flip a nylon rope around her neck.

"Open the gate at the back of the truck," Tomas yelled up to Arnoldo and Jamie. "Then step away from it. I don't want this beast jumping out on top of you!"

The two of them scrambled down from the catwalk.

"Ready!" Arnoldo shouted to his uncle, sliding the truck gate wide open.

"Here we come!" Tomas called back.

Eyes wide with terror, Jamie's filly flew up the alley, dragging the nylon rope behind her.

She didn't seem to notice where she was headed—she just wanted to get away from her tormentors. She bounded up the loading chute and clattered into the back of the truck with no hesitation . . . at all. *Wham!* The buckskin filly crashed straight into the wooden planking. She shook her head, stunned, and Tomas slid the gate shut behind her and fastened it with a heavy chain.

"Can you see the rope, Chuy?"

The younger man reached cautiously between the two lowest planks. He grabbed the end of the nylon rope that was looped around the filly's neck.

Jamie peered between the planks herself. The horse was dark with sweat, her sides heaving.

Jamie glanced up at the sun, almost overhead now. "She could have a heat stroke!" she said to Arnoldo.

"Or we will," Tomas said. He had a long scratch down his left arm. Chuy's once-white T-shirt was ripped where he'd caught it on a fence, and he was covered with dirt. The third guy was limping. All three of them were breathing hard and soaked with perspiration.

Tomas wiped his sweaty face with his arm and sized up the situation.

Suddenly the filly reared, pulling on the rope and almost jerking Chuy over. She pawed noisily at the planking.

"She's gonna crawl out while you're on the highway," Chuy said, hanging on as best he could.

"Or hurt herself trying to," the third guy said, grabbing hold of the rope, too, to pull the filly's head down.

"Would it help to cover up her eyes?" Jamie asked.

Chuy looked doubtful.

Tomas nodded at Jamie. "If this horse can't see where she's going . . . maybe she'll stay put."

He found another navy T-shirt in his truck cab. It took all three men several minutes to drag the filly into a corner, close to the planking. Then Tomas climbed up to plunk the T-shirt over her head. The horse's muscles shivered—they looked ready to burst through her skin. But she stood still.

He knotted the nylon rope up short to the planking, then jumped down and hurriedly shook hands with Chuy and the other man. "Thanks, guys—we'd better get moving."

Jamie and Arnoldo slid into the truck cab. Tomas stuck the key in the ignition. With the first rumbling of the engine, the filly started struggling again.

Jamie squinted through the back window of the truck. The horse was flexing her powerful neck, but she couldn't snap the nylon rope. She just pulled the noose tighter.

"She'll choke!"

"If the rope cuts off her wind, she'll stop fighting it." Tomas eased the truck through the parking lot.

He drove slowly, trying not to jostle the passenger in back, so the trip seemed to take hours. The horse fought the rope most of the way, her hoofs sliding and clattering on the truck bed.

Jamie breathed a sigh of relief when they reached the cattle guard into the ranch. "There's a loading chute at the far side of the corral," she told Tomas as they rolled down the dirt road.

"Then that's where we'll jump the horse out of the truck."

They rattled past the ranch house. Jamie crossed her fingers, hoping that her grandfather wouldn't see or hear them, not until her horse was safely unloaded and less jittery.

But Arnoldo murmured, "Uh-oh—here he comes, Jamie."

Walt Cameron was charging toward them, the screen door hanging open behind him.

Tomas glanced into his side mirror. "The man doesn't look happy." But he kept driving, past the windmill and the barn, around the corral and the two smaller pens to the loading chute.

"Step on it, Tío!" Arnoldo said urgently.

Tomas backed the truck up until it bumped against the chute. He leaped out to slide open the wooden gate.

The kids scrambled out of the truck, too. Jamie closed the

east and west gates of the corral—old Samson was grazing in the pasture, out of harm's way. Then she climbed to the top of the fence.

While Arnoldo looked out for Walt Cameron, Tomas scaled the truck's planking to rip the T-shirt off the filly's head.

As soon as she could see again, she squealed loudly, glared at Tomas with her ears back, and fought the rope. She was threatening to knock him off his plank, but he reached into the pocket of his jeans for a knife. He cut the nylon rope with a single swipe and pulled it away from her neck.

"You are one lucky lady!" Tomas said, waving the piece of rope at her. "Go for it—you're home."

The buckskin filly didn't move for several seconds, not realizing she was free. Then she lunged through the open gate at the back of the truck, galloped down the loading chute, and bolted into the corral. She raced to the far end of the long pen before turning to face them.

"Your granddad!" Arnoldo hissed at Jamie.

Walt Cameron was steaming around the side of the barn. "What's all this?" he thundered.

Jamie met her grandfather halfway.

"I . . . uh . . . actually, I . . . bought this horse."

"You bought a horse?" her grandfather said in disbelief.

"At the auction. I used my—"

"Your summer money," he said, catching on all too quickly.

He gazed over the fence at Jamie's horse, who was watching

them warily from the far end of the corral.

"Anderson Ranch," Mr. Cameron said. "Don't you know they'd never sell one of their horses at a cattle auction unless it was worthless? Crippled. Or an outlaw."

He was so certain he'd hit the nail on the head that he nodded a few times.

"She's just scared," Jamie said as positively as she could. "As soon as she cools off . . ."

"You should know better, Tomas," her granddad said sternly to Arnoldo's uncle, standing next to his truck. "You grew up around horses."

"I just provided the transportation, Mr. Cameron," Tomas said easily. "Speaking of transportation, have you ever thought about laying some gravel down on your road? It could sure save you some money on truck repairs. Hey, we better pick up those bikes, Arnoldo," he added.

"Yeah, see you, Jamie." In a low voice Arnoldo said, "I'll call you later."

"Thanks for . . . "

"No sweat." He jumped into the truck, and Tomas and Arnoldo rumbled away, glad to get out of there.

Mr. Cameron took one last look at the filly, then headed toward the house, leaving Jamie alone with her problem.

The filly was quiet beneath the lacy leaves of a mesquite tree. But she was still on her guard—she was staring straight at Jamie.

As Jamie took a couple of careful steps down the fence in her direction, the filly snorted, pricked her ears, and eased back a few yards.

"Okay, I won't crowd you," Jamie murmured, leaning her forehead against the fence. "But I will give you a name."

What was it going to be? The horses at the stable in Maine had names like Quest and Royal and King.

Then Uncle Tomas's voice floated into Jamie's brain: "You are one lucky lady," he'd said to the filly.

"I'll call you Lucky Lady," Jamie decided. "Maybe that'll bring some luck to both of us, because we're going to need it."

5

$\mathcal{J}$ AMIE MADE SURE THE WATER TROUGH WAS FULL
before she trudged to the ranch house herself.

Her granddad was sitting at the kitchen table. "I'll borrow
a trailer from my neighbor, and we'll run the filly through the
auction again next week," he said. "At least you'll make some
of your money back."

"But I don't want to sell her!" Lucky Lady was hers now.
She'd saved the filly from certain death, and Jamie was going
to see to it that nothing else bad ever happened to her.

"You're as hardheaded as your mother!" her grandfather thundered.

What about YOU? Jamie yelled in her head.

"How do you intend to feed her? Hay and oats cost money."

Jamie glanced around the kitchen. "I'll trade you painting this . . . this grungy room for horse feed."

Her granddad didn't seem to hear. "What happens when you leave in two months? I'm not keeping an outlaw on the place—I'm too old to fool with one."

"She's not an outlaw, and I'll be riding her long before two months have passed." *Why did I say that?* "I'll ride her all the way to Maine if I have to!"

Her grandfather shook his head. "Then you'll ride her without my help." He pushed his chair back and walked to the screen door. "I'm going into town—you can fix yourself a sandwich."

As Jamie watched him climb into his truck, she thought, *Guess what? I don't want to look at you right now, either!*

Once he'd driven away from the house, she went outside to check on her horse. Lucky Lady was nibbling at a clump of grass near the water trough. As soon as she spotted Jamie, she trotted toward the mesquite tree.

"It's too hot to do anything," Jamie called after her, "but you'll have to get used to me fast, Lucky."

The buckskin filly shook her head, tossing her black mane.

"Yes, you will," Jamie added firmly, imagining herself galloping Lucky across the pasture, the wind in their faces.

Not that she had a clue where to begin.

I wish Mom were here—she'd show me how to get started.

Jamie couldn't eat more than half a turkey sandwich—she was too wound up. She was flipping channels on the TV set in the living room, looking for news about Southeast Asia—as close as she'd be to her mother for a while—when the screen door in the kitchen creaked open.

"You might as well get going," her grandfather said.

Had he changed his mind about Lucky? She switched off the TV and stood up, suddenly hopeful.

But he set two cans of white paint down on the kitchen floor, and pulled a roller out of a paper bag and handed it to Jamie.

"One coat on the walls in here will pay for hay for a month. Start over by the window," he directed, "while I patch this crack in the plasterboard."

"What about oats?"

Her granddad pried open a paint can. "Well . . . a fifty-pound bag of oats costs six something, and a horse eats around ten pounds of oats a day. A forty-pound bale of hay is four dollars, and a horse'll eat ten pounds of that, too."

"So what's it come to?" Jamie asked, too frazzled to figure it all out.

"Two or three dollars a day to feed that filly," said her granddad. "About sixty dollars a month. So a second coat of paint in here, and a first coat in your mother's room, will cover a couple of months of hay and some of the oats, too."

What about when she left for Maine? Jamie didn't want to think about that, not yet. She reached into the bag for a paper paint cap and stuck it on her head. "It's a deal."

Jamie finished painting the walls in the kitchen in a couple of hours. Then she helped her grandfather take down the glass cases and the trophies in the spare room so that she could start working in there.

She was pretty certain the temperature inside the house had risen well past the one-hundred-thirteen-degree mark Arnoldo had told her about. Beads of sweat were dripping off the tip of her nose when her grandfather finally said, "Go outside and cool off while I empty these bookcases and move them into the living room."

It *was* cooler outside—a soft breeze was blowing inland from the Gulf.

Jamie pulled off her paint cap and headed for the corral.

Lucky Lady was dozing at the shady end, under the mesquite tree, one hind foot resting on its toe. As Jamie got closer, however, the filly went on the alert, shifting uncertainly.

Jamie had read about a man who studied Arctic wolves. For weeks, he'd lain near the edge of the pack without moving a muscle, until the wolves realized he wasn't dangerous. Little by little, they came to accept and even approach him.

This horse wasn't nearly as wild as an Arctic wolf. And Jamie had to start somewhere . . .

She picked up a bucket and quietly opened the east gate. She took a step into the corral, latching the gate behind her.

Lucky Lady snorted loudly, her eyes fixed on Jamie.

Jamie remained totally still for a couple of minutes, clutching the bucket, until the horse had relaxed enough to switch her tail at the flies buzzing around her. But as soon as Jamie took another step, Lucky bounded away, racing down the far side of the corral to the opposite end.

"You're gonna get hot out there in the sun, Lucky."

Jamie set the bucket down near the water trough, sat on it, and waited. She avoided looking at Lucky Lady straight on. Instead, she studied the ground in front of her.

A shiny black beetle was rolling a ball of dung along with its hind feet, hurrying to retrieve it when it escaped down the hollow of a hoof print.

Large red ants swarmed all over a dead lizard. Beyond them, Jamie spotted an S-curved track left by a snake in the sand. Forked footprints of a roadrunner zigzagged back and forth across the corral.

Then a hawk screamed high overhead. As Jamie glanced skyward, she caught sight of something out of the corner of her eye. The buckskin filly was edging up the fence, glancing warily at the strange human near the water trough, then over at her spot under the mesquite, and back at Jamie.

Jamie sat without moving, hoping the horse might be curious enough to come closer. But as soon as Lucky drew even with her, the filly bolted, racing down the fence to her tree at the shady end of the corral.

Jamie sighed. *If I move toward her, she'll stampede. And if I just sit here, weeks could pass, I'll go home, and Granddad will sell her for sure!*

Suddenly she heard a shrill whinny. Samson was galloping heavily across the pasture toward the corral.

There was an answering whinny from the buckskin filly, and she trotted toward the fence.

Jamie scrambled to her feet, afraid that Lucky might charge the old sorrel horse. But the two of them touched noses gently and nickered their greetings.

Although Samson was a couple of hands taller than Lucky Lady, the filly was already almost as heavily muscled as he was. The horses walked toward the shade of the big mesquite tree, making soft, whispering noises, and staying as close to each other as they could with a fence in between them.

That's when Jamie had an idea: *What if I put Samson in the corral, too? I'll pat him and brush him, and Lucky will see that I'm not dangerous.*

The horses were in a huddle near the tree. Jamie hurried quickly across the corral to the west gate, unlatched it, and threw it open.

Both horses turned, and Samson took a few steps in her direction.

"Come on, boy." Jamie walked through the gate. "You can visit her up close in the corral, and . . . hey!"

She'd counted on Lucky staying well away from her, at the far end of the pen. But in the blink of an eye the filly charged down the fence and dodged through the open gate, passing so close to Jamie that she felt the warmth of the horse's body for just a moment.

Seconds later, Lucky was tearing across the pasture, with old Samson galloping after her, whinnying worriedly.

"No-o-o-o!" Jamie yelled as they disappeared into a thicket of scrubby mesquites. "You jerk! You'll never be able to catch her now!" she told herself, and burst into angry tears.

6

$\mathscr{J}$AMIE WAS LEANING AGAINST THE OPEN GATE, CRY-
ing because she was so angry with herself and scared
for the horses, when she heard her granddad shout, "Jamie?"

He was sprinting toward her—she'd never seen him move
so fast! His face looked dark and furious.

But he didn't yell when he reached her. Instead, he
grabbed her by the shoulders: "Are . . . are you . . . " It took him
a moment to catch his breath, and she realized he was frightened for her.

"I'm okay," she said tearfully. "Lucky's gone! I thought I could use Samson to get her to come to me." She swiped at her eyes with the back of her hand. "What if she steps in a gopher hole out there and breaks her leg or gets hung in a barbed-wire fence?"

"If Samson's with the filly, you don't have to worry about her too much. He'll steady her down."

"But how will I ever catch her?" she murmured, mostly to herself, because she didn't really expect her grandfather to help her.

"Not by chasing her around the pasture. Wait for her to come in on her own."

"Oh, sure." No way that was going to happen.

"Think like a horse." He walked out of the corral with Jamie at his side. "Samson won't come back this evening because the filly's all riled up, and he'll stay with her. By tomorrow morning, he'll be eager for his bucket of oats. He'll walk into the pen and start eating, and the filly will follow him, because horses like to stay together. And you'll slam the gate closed behind them."

Mr. Cameron pulled open the screen door and steered Jamie into the house.

That evening Arnoldo called.

"You missed a giant brush fire!" he said. "It started behind the auction barn around three o'clock and burned all the way to the county line! Fire trucks came from five towns. Didn't you see the smoke?"

"Uh-uh . . . I . . . uh . . ." Her grandfather was sitting at the other end of the couch, watching a ball game.

"He's right there, he can hear you, and he's still mad about you buying that horse?" Arnoldo guessed.

"Yes, but . . . worse than that—Lucky got away," Jamie whispered hurriedly as her granddad headed into the kitchen for a Coke.

"How? Where'd she go?"

"She's in the pasture somewhere, and it was my own dumb fault—I let her run out the gate."

"We could look for her in my dad's Jeep," Arnoldo offered. "He lets me drive it off road."

"Thanks, Arnoldo. But Granddad thinks Samson will bring her with him when he comes in to eat tomorrow morning," Jamie said.

"You're calling her Lucky?"

"Lucky Lady," said Jamie. Suddenly she felt so exhausted by everything that had happened that day, she could hardly speak. "I'd better go."

"Okay—later," said Arnoldo.

"I haven't forgotten I owe you two-fifty."

"Don't worry about it."

They hung up.

◆　　◆　　◆

Jamie went to bed early and dreamed that she and Lucky had run all the way to Maine. They were swimming out into the Atlantic, headed for England, when Jamie's granddad woke her up. It was daybreak.

"Get dressed. And put these on."

He handed her a pair of brand-new, black leather cowboy boots.

He must have bought them the afternoon before, when he went to town. Which was after Lucky, so maybe he wasn't really that angry with her.

"Wow—thanks a lot, Granddad."

"What would I tell your mother if you got a snakebite?" he muttered gruffly. "It's cool right now, and the rattlesnakes are crawling."

Jamie jumped into her clothes, pulled on the new boots— they fit fine with her thickest socks—and hurried outside.

Her grandfather had filled two buckets with oats from the barn. A coiled rope was slung over his shoulder.

"The horses will be waking up right about now, so they'll come in for water soon. Samson'll have his mind on these oats—and we'll be ready."

He set the buckets down under the mesquite tree and opened the west gate of the corral. Then he tied one end of his rope to the frame of the gate.

He stretched the rest of the rope out flat on the ground, across the gap left by the opened gate, and along the fence line.

"What do I do?" Jamie asked.

"I want you to hide behind this bush." He pointed to a thorny shrub speckled with red berries. "I'm too stiff to hunker down and the horses would see me, so I'll stand behind the loading chute."

Jamie understood. "I'll have the loose end of the rope in my hand. And when the horses walk into the corral, I'll pull on it and swing the gate closed."

"That's it," said her grandfather. "I'll yell when they're far enough inside so the filly can't spin around and run out again. Then you'll jerk on the rope. I'll tie the gate closed."

Jamie crouched behind the thorny bush, clutching the end of the long rope with both hands. She couldn't see her granddad, but she knew he was waiting, too, and watching for the horses.

She took a deep breath to calm herself, and breathed in the spicy smell of the dry weeds and grasses around her. The air was perfectly still; the world was quiet. Birds were just beginning to chirp sleepily.

I wouldn't mind living in Texas. Part of the reason her mom had left was because she wanted to see new places and do new things. But all this was new to Jamie. She could find plenty of stuff to do—just learning about horses could keep her busy for years!

Her mother and her grandfather just naturally rubbed each other the wrong way. Could it be that they were too much alike? But they cared about each other—she knew they did.

Suddenly Jamie was smiling.

"Think of things you can do together," her mom had said to her on the phone.

Well, Granddad and I are definitely doing things together now.

And she was pretty sure he'd been keeping a sharp eye on her—he'd appeared out of nowhere, seconds after the filly ran away. So he *was* involved, in spite of what he'd said about Jamie being on her own with this horse.

Suddenly she heard a soft whinny.

They're coming . . . She gripped the rope as tightly as she could, ready to pull. But a minute or two passed with no sign of the horses, and Jamie got antsier. Where were they? And what if it was just Samson? Lucky Lady could be hurt somewhere—lame or hung up in a fence or . . .

She heard the thud of hoofs on sandy ground, louder than a single horse, wasn't it? Finally she spotted a dark patch, and then a light one, moving past the tangle of thorny twigs that hid her. Jamie waited. . . .

"Do it!" her grandfather shouted.

She shot to her feet and jerked on the rope, her hands taking up the slack.

Lucky Lady pivoted on her back feet as soon as the gate swung forward. But she was fifteen feet inside the corral, and Jamie's granddad was running toward her, waving his arms in the air and whooping and hollering. He drove Lucky back from the gate, and it closed, banging against the post.

"We did it!" Jamie yelled, bouncing around. "Thanks, Granddad. Thanks so much for helping me."

In the corral, Samson headed straight for his bucket of oats, completely unconcerned with what was going on.

Lucky galloped past him, her tail in the air. She felt safer when she put the old sorrel horse between herself and the humans.

"I'm hungry," Jamie's grandfather said abruptly. "Let's get some breakfast."

They drove into Wilcox, to Marie's Café just off Main Street. Jamie ordered scrambled eggs and *pan de polvo*, a Mexican sweet roll, and her granddad ordered fried eggs and bacon. They were eating when a man in a gray cowboy hat stopped at their table.

"Walt," the man said, shaking hands with Mr. Cameron. "Isn't this the little lady who bought that outlaw filly at the auction?"

Jamie recognized him, too—the guy who'd sat behind her and Arnoldo in the bleachers.

"This is my granddaughter, Jamie Cooper," Mr. Cameron said. "Jamie, Bill Norris."

"Hello, Jamie." He tipped his hat.

"I wouldn't call the filly an outlaw."

Jamie turned to stare at her granddad.

lucky lady • 5 5

He went on, "She's just a green two-year-old that's probably been mistreated more than once, the way the Andersons break horses. A little attention, and . . ."

"Does that mean you're working with her, Walt?" Bill Norris shook his head. "Uh-uh. Maybe if you were in your prime, forty years ago. I heard she hurt somebody bad over there," he added. "If Jamie were my grandkid, I wouldn't want her in the same county with that filly—I'd get rid of her right away."

He walked to the front of the café to pay his bill.

Jamie glanced at her granddad, her heart pounding. If Lucky had really hurt someone . . .

"What Bill Norris knows about horses would fit on this, with room to spare," Mr. Cameron said, tearing open a sugar packet for his coffee.

Which wasn't exactly a no to getting rid of the filly. But it wasn't exactly a yes to keeping her, either.

7

$\mathcal{W}$HEN JAMIE AND HER GRANDDAD WENT GROCERY
shopping that morning, she added a couple of pack-
ages of carrots to the cart.

At the ranch, she stuffed carrots into the pockets of her
jeans. She grabbed a currycomb out of the barn, and headed
for the corral. Instead of opening a gate this time, though,
Jamie climbed the fence—she wasn't taking any chances.

The two horses were asleep under the mesquite tree, heads
to tails to swat flies. As soon as Jamie's boots hit the ground

inside the corral, Lucky edged away.

But Samson nickered expectantly, hoping she had some treats for him.

"I've got carrots," she called to the old sorrel horse. She pulled one out of her pocket and chewed loudly on the end of it to encourage him.

He ambled toward her, his eyes fixed on the tasty vegetable in her hand. When he was close enough, he stretched out his neck and grabbed the carrot with his long yellow teeth, nodding happily as he crunched.

"Good boy." Jamie patted Samson's cheek and fed him a second carrot.

Then she started brushing his neck with sweeping strokes of the currycomb.

Lucky Lady was watching. The buckskin filly hadn't moved from the shady end of the corral, but she was following the whole procedure.

"Doesn't this feel g-o-ood, Samson?"

Humming softly, Jamie worked along his neck with the currycomb, onto his left shoulder, and down to his chest.

Small clouds of dust rose with each stroke, and bits of grass and the seedheads of weeds fell to the ground.

"You guys rolled in the dirt, didn't you? You were having a great time, running wild out there in the pasture."

She brushed him until his left side gleamed like honey. Ducking under his neck to start on his right side, she gasped.

Lucky Lady was standing not ten feet away from her—the plan was working!

But Jamie pretended she didn't notice. She reached into her back pocket for another carrot and held it just far enough in front of Samson's nose to make him step toward it.

Slowly, she edged the old horse around until she was facing Lucky, with Samson in between them. Now, while she worked on him, she could inspect the buckskin filly.

There were a couple of scratches on Lucky's nose, and her neck was scraped raw where she'd fought the rope in Tomas's truck. Then Jamie spotted a deep gash across her lower ribs. The hair had been sliced away to reveal a half-healed wound, in the right place for a gouge from a sharp spur.

I'll never do anything to hurt you, Lucky, Jamie promised her silently.

The filly took a couple of cautious steps closer to Samson. When she realized that Jamie was looking at her over his back, however, she whuffed and trotted away, to watch from a safer distance.

Disappointed, Jamie patted the old horse on the flank. "I guess that's it for now, Samson."

She wedged the currycomb into the top of her jeans and walked to the trough to splash her hot face with water.

When she turned around, Samson was standing right behind her. And Lucky Lady was staring over his rump.

Jamie sank slowly onto the bucket she'd left beside the

trough the day before, pulled another carrot out of her pocket, and handed it to Samson.

He finished it in three loud bites. When no more treats appeared, he plodded to the far side of the trough, sank his head into water up to his eyes, and started grazing on the moss that grew on the bottom.

Jamie was afraid Lucky would bolt without Samson for protection. But the buckskin filly stayed put. She was close— if Jamie took two giant steps, she'd be touching her.

Jamie made herself sit still, gazed down at the toes of her boots, and listened to the windmill creaking as it spun slowly in the breeze. She could hear her granddad rummaging around in the barn. Crows cawed in the trees next to the ranch house. A locust buzzed somewhere near . . .

Cautiously, Jamie peered up at Lucky. The filly's head was lowered, and her ears were pointed right at Jamie. In fact, she seemed to be staring at Jamie's new boots.

Jamie noticed that the muscles in Lucky's front legs were quivering, which made her uneasy . . .

Suddenly, Lucky squealed and reared straight up!

For a split second, Jamie saw the filly's front feet pawing the air high over her head.

She's crazy! Jamie thought, if she thought anything at all before she threw herself sideways off the bucket. She rolled once, then scrambled to the fence. She climbed to the top rail without taking a breath.

Lucky had slammed her front feet to the ground right where Jamie had been sitting. She reared again, then her front hooves smashed down on the bucket.

Jamie was frozen on the top fence rail. She couldn't seem to make herself move . . .

"Jamie, get down from there!" Her granddad was only a few steps away.

He grabbed hold of her arms and lifted her down on the far side of the fence. "What happened? Are you hurt?"

"I'm okay, Granddad," she said shakily.

He thundered, "I'm getting rid of that animal this very afternoon!"

Jamie was too scared to argue with him. In fact, she wasn't sure she even *wanted* to argue.

Lucky had her nose to the ground, and she was edging cautiously toward the mangled bucket . . .

"Hold on—what has she got there?" As Jamie's granddad moved closer to the fence, the filly backed away from him and trotted across the corral.

He was staring at the ground near to the water trough. "It's a rattlesnake," he said at last.

"A r-rattlesnake?" Jamie stammered, not making sense of his words.

"She killed it, right beside the bucket." He climbed the fence and scooped up a dead diamondback with the toe of his boot. The four-foot-long snake had a dozen or so rattles on its tail and a bulge in its stomach. Its head was crushed.

"It was probably trying to keep cool in the shade of the trough," Mr. Cameron said. "You sat down almost on top of it."

"It c-could have bitten me!" Jamie said, shivering, and she remembered. "I—I did hear a buzzing sound. I thought it was a locust, and . . ."

"Lucky knew what it was," said her granddad, using the filly's name for the first time. She was standing in her spot under the mesquite tree, watching them closely.

"Why'd she kill it?" Jamie asked. "Why didn't she run away?"

"Some horses just naturally hate snakes more than others," her grandfather answered. "You were just lucky."

Lucky Lady.

8

JAMIE AND HER GRANDDAD WERE HAVING LUNCH IN the freshly painted kitchen when the phone rang.

Jamie wondered if it was her mom calling, but she heard her granddad say, "Hello, Gloria . . . Yes, I believe she'd like that. . . . I'll drop her off in a couple of hours. Thanks."

"That was Arnoldo Ochoa's mother," he said as he sat down at the kitchen table again. "She asked if you'd like to go swimming this afternoon."

"But, Granddad," Jamie said, "what about Lucky Lady? I have to . . ."

"I'll keep an eye on her while you're gone."

Jamie was startled by his offer.

But a swim might stop the rattlesnake replay in her brain.

"Well . . . okay," she said.

Around 2:30, Jamie put her bathing suit on under shorts and a tank top and slipped into her sandals, then she and her granddad drove into Wilcox.

Mr. Cameron made a right turn off Main Street. They rolled past the old plaza, around the white-stucco Catholic church with its blue-tiled bell towers, turned left, and stopped outside a yellow frame house with a wagon-wheel fence.

The front door of the house flew open, and Arnoldo barreled down the steps. A small spotted dog bounced along behind him, barking at the top of its lungs.

Arnoldo jerked open Jamie's door. "Hey, Jamie!" He shouted to make himself heard over the dog.

"Hi, Mr. Cameron," he added more quietly, before yelling to Jamie, "Come around to the pool!"

"Bye," Jamie said to her granddad.

"We'll drive her home!" Arnoldo told him. "Chester, shut up! Isn't he excellent? My cousin Ernie gave him to us a couple of weeks ago."

Arnoldo and Chester led Jamie through a cactus garden

and around a birdbath, into the backyard.

"Great pool!" she exclaimed.

The bright blue water was edged with rocks, so it looked almost like a real pond. There was a big boulder to use as a diving board.

"Check this out." Arnoldo flipped a switch on the side of the house, and Jamie heard water gurgling. A little waterfall flowed down a group of large rocks into the pool.

"That is so cool!" Jamie had to raise her voice because Chester was barking at the waterfall, and she began to understand why Arnoldo's cousin might have decided to give the dog away.

"My dad did all the wiring, put together the filter and the pump for the waterfall, and Uncle Tomas poured the concrete and laid the rocks," Arnoldo was saying. "Where's your suit?"

"I'm already wearing it." She couldn't wait to dive in.

"I'll change. Come inside and meet my mom."

"And your brother." A slender woman with short curly hair had opened the sliding glass door onto the patio. "Hi, Jamie—I'm Gloria Ochoa, Arnoldo's mom."

"Thanks very much for asking me over." Jamie stepped into a large open kitchen painted bright blue, with yellow cabinets and countertops. A small piñata in the shape of a rooster hung from the ceiling lamp.

"Our pleasure to have you. This is David, Arnoldo's little brother," Mrs. Ochoa said.

A toddler with a round face and black eyes grinned at Jamie from a playpen in the center of the room.

"Hi, David," Jamie said, kneeling down in front of the playpen.

"Watch his hands," Arnoldo warned, heading for his room. "If he gets hold of your hair, he'll never turn you loose."

"Are you enjoying your visit, Jamie?" Mrs. Ochoa asked, offering her a glass of iced tea.

"It's been . . . interesting so far."

"Arnoldo told me about your wild horse," Mrs. Ochoa said, smiling.

Her son burst into the kitchen again, wearing a dark-green swimsuit. He threw a towel to Jamie before sliding the door open and racing down the blistering-hot sidewalk muttering "Ouch, ouch, ouch," with every barefooted step he took.

Chester was nipping at Arnoldo's heels as he cannonballed into the pool. The little dog did a racing dive right behind him.

Jamie burst out laughing as Chester smacked the water a couple of feet away from the edge and paddled furiously after Arnoldo.

She kicked off her sandals, peeled off her shorts and tank top, and dove in herself. The water was perfect, just cool enough to feel tingly.

"It's always freezing in Maine," she told Arnoldo when she surfaced. "You absolutely can't swim in the ocean, not without a wet suit. The lakes are almost as cold. And if pools aren't indoors or heated, you can only use them about four weeks a year."

"Move down here—you can swim for nine or ten months," Arnoldo said, scooping Chester out of the water and setting him down in the grass. "He's so crazy he'll wear himself out."

Jamie and Arnoldo swam laps and raced a couple of times. She beat him in the backstroke, and they tied in the crawl.

They were taking turns jumping off the diving boulder when Arnoldo said, "There's my granddad."

A stooped little man with white hair and glasses had walked out of the house. He sat down in a lawn chair in the shade of a tree, and a very wet Chester jumped into his lap.

"Abuelito, esta muchacha es la nieta de señor Cameron," Arnoldo called out. *"Se llama Jamie."*

"Hello!" Arnoldo's granddad said, waving to Jamie.

"Hello!" said Jamie, waving back.

"He doesn't speak much English, but he knows a lot about horses—he worked on a ranch for most of his life. You want to talk to him about training Lucky?"

"Sure." She'd take any advice she could get.

But Mr. Ochoa knew only one way to break horses.

"He says that you rope 'em out of the herd and tie 'em up," Arnoldo translated for him.

Mr. Ochoa spoke again.

"You rub 'em with burlap sacks to get them used to having something touch their backs."

"Lucky Lady would jump straight over the fence if I ever waved a sack at her," Jamie said.

Mr. Ochoa talked some more, and Arnoldo repeated in English: "When you're ready to ride, you saddle the horse, tie one of his back legs up real tight, and jump on him. After a while you turn the leg loose, and let the horse buck till he's totally wasted. And that's how you tame 'em—show 'em who's boss."

Jamie thought of the deep gash across Lucky's ribs—maybe she wasn't the kind of horse who'd put up with being treated so harshly.

"Please tell your granddad thank you—*muchas gracias*." Which was all the Spanish Jamie knew.

Mr. Ochoa nodded and smiled at her.

"But you don't want to do it that way, right?" Arnoldo guessed.

"I couldn't do all that by myself," Jamie said.

Arnoldo's granddad added something as they were lowering themselves back into the pool.

"He says you should ask your grandfather. When he was younger, he was one of the best in the country with colts."

It was the second time that day that someone had mentioned him training colts: first Mr. Norris, and now Mr. Ochoa.

She was really sorry that he was too old for Lucky.

9

ARNOLDO AND HIS DAD DROVE JAMIE HOME around six, along with Junior's bike retrieved from the auction barn.

Her grandfather opened the screen door for her. "You're red as a beet."

"I thought if I stayed in the water I wouldn't burn. . . ." Jamie said, flinching when she touched one of her seared legs.

She didn't sleep well that night, partly because she was worried about making some headway with Lucky Lady and partly because she was so sunburned that she couldn't get comfortable.

Her legs, arms, and shoulders were a sizzling red, and they felt as if they were on fire. Even the sheets hurt where they touched her skin.

Her granddad took one look at her the next morning and said, "I'm going into town to find you something to put on that sunburn."

Jamie groaned while she eased herself down onto a kitchen chair. "And could you buy more carrots, please?"

As Jamie walked to the corral with the carrots, she stared down at the ground all the way, checking for snakes. She was too sore to climb the fence, so she let herself in through the east gate, and latched it behind her.

Lucky Lady and Samson were standing together under the mesquite.

Jamie sat down on one of the stumps that braced the gate— she did not want to get anywhere near the water trough.

"Good morning, guys," she said casually, holding out a carrot.

Neither horse was hungry—they'd each eaten a bucket of oats. But Jamie knew Samson could never turn down a treat.

Sure enough, he plodded over to grab a carrot.

Lucky followed him, lifting her head and studying Jamie intently.

"I've got one for you, too," Jamie murmured to her over Samson's enthusiastic crunching.

When she held a carrot out to the filly, Lucky edged toward her. Jamie could see her dark eyelashes and a small pink triangle on the tip of her nose that she hadn't noticed before.

But Lucky ignored the treat—her nose came to rest on Jamie's sunburned wrist.

She's going to bite me . . . Jamie forced herself to keep still.

Lucky's stiff whiskers moved up her arm as the filly sniffed and snuffled. And suddenly a thick, warm, wet tongue rested for a few seconds on Jamie's skin, just below her shirt sleeve.

Lucky liked the sunburn cream! Probably no one had ever thought of using it as a horse-training aid. Jamie worked hard not to giggle.

The filly licked her arm again, slowly. Then Lucky raised her head until her nose touched Jamie's hair. She nibbled at Jamie's hairline with her lips.

"Yuck—you're drooling on me, Lucky," Jamie said aloud.

At the sound of her voice, the filly backed away. But she paused beside Samson's left flank, still watching Jamie.

As soon as Jamie stood up, though, Lucky trotted to the center of the corral.

Jamie went to the barn for a currycomb. When she started brushing Samson, Lucky Lady lingered about five yards from them.

As Jamie hunkered down to brush the sorrel's front leg, something nudged her shoulder.

Lucky Lady was standing next to Samson's flank again. She'd stretched out her neck, and her nose was bumping against Jamie's brushing arm.

Carefully, Jamie turned the currycomb around so that it faced Lucky's nose. The filly sniffed at it for a moment.

Jamie was sliding the currycomb gently down the filly's cheek when Lucky turned tail and ran to the safety of her mesquite tree. She'd spotted Mr. Cameron walking toward the corral.

"I have to check the windmill in the next pasture," he told Jamie. "I don't want you working with that horse if I'm not around."

"Can I go with you?"

Her grandfather nodded.

He threw a couple of heavy wrenches into the back of his truck, and he and Jamie climbed into the cab. They bumped along the dirt road for about a mile, until they reached an iron gate over a cattle guard.

"Just leave it open," he told her, stopping the truck.

Cows and calves grazed farther out in the pasture, the first Jamie had seen since she arrived. Her granddad's cattle had been cross-bred Brahmans, gray or white, with dangling ears, large humps, and long, graceful legs. These cows were dark red and heavily built.

When Jamie got back in the truck, she asked, "What kind of cattle are those?"

"The man who leases from me, Riley Yates, raises registered Santa Gertrudis—expensive hobby," Mr. Cameron told her. "There's the windmill."

The big metal wheel at the top of the steel tower wasn't turning at all.

He forced the truck straight through a mesquite thicket, and parked between the tower and an earthen barrier about four feet high. He and Jamie climbed out.

"This is the dam for a stock tank. It catches water from the windmill and traps any rainwater that happens along." He picked up the larger wrench from the back of the truck. "I brought you here once to fish for snapping turtles."

He started to scale the windmill tower.

Jamie didn't remember the place, or ever fishing with her grandfather. She walked to the top of the earthen dam. On the far side of it, the land sloped just enough to allow a wide, shallow lake to form. Dozens of frogs were lined up on the muddy banks, light green ones with darker spots.

"How deep is it?" Jamie called to her grandfather, now sitting on the tiny platform just below the silver blades of the windmill.

"Around four feet," he called back.

A couple of turtles had poked their heads out of the pond. Dragonflies hovered in the steamy air above it.

She was enjoying the sight of a large pool of water in such a dry landscape when suddenly she *did* remember. She'd been around five or six years old, and they'd fished for turtles together, using string and a nail threaded with pieces of raw bacon. They'd even caught a few snappers, then turned them loose to crawl into the pond again. She'd had a great time that day, just hanging out with her granddad.

Metal screeched against metal behind her—he was tightening a gear. The blades started to turn. All at once, water gushed into the stock tank from a rusty pipe almost buried in the mud at the near end.

"I'm done, Jamie." Her grandfather started down the windmill tower. "Get in the truck, before you burn worse."

As they headed for the ranch again, Jamie asked, "Would it be all right with Mr. Yates if I showed the stock tank to Arnoldo?"

"I leased this ranch to Mr. Yates, I didn't sell it to him. You can take Arnoldo whenever you want."

Jamie worked with Lucky for the next few mornings. In the afternoons, she painted the kitchen walls a second time, and started on the ceiling. She rolled a first coat of sky-blue paint on the walls in the spare room as well—blue was her mom's favorite color.

"You can't breathe these fumes all night long," her grandfather said as he inspected her work. "Put your sheets on the couch."

That night she was asleep in the living room, dreaming that she'd ridden Lucky to Wilcox to see Arnoldo, when the phone rang right next to her head.

She fumbled for it groggily. "Hello?"

"Jamie, is that you?" It was her mother's voice.

"Mom!" Jamie was wide awake now.

"How did you get to the phone so fast?"

"I'm sleeping in the living room because I just painted your room and it's still smelly in there," Jamie said.

"Has Dad put you to work?"

Jamie cleared her throat. "Kind of—it's to pay for horse feed."

"What do you need horse feed for?"

"Because I have a horse, Mom. I used the money you gave me to buy her." Jamie blurted it out.

She expected her mother to scold: "You've spent all of your money?"

Instead she said, "Jamie, what kind of horse can you buy for two hundred dollars?"

Sometimes Jamie forgot how much her mom knew about horses.

"I wish you could see her, Mom! She's cream colored, with black legs and a black mane and tail. She's just a two-year-old, so—"

"What's wrong with her?" her mom interrupted. "Two hundred dollars is barely enough to buy a goat these days."

"Well, she's not exactly . . . trained," Jamie said.

"Meaning?"

"I can't ride her yet. But she'll let me touch her now, and haltering's next."

She left out the part about the rattlesnake, although it might have put Lucky in a better light. She didn't want to give her mother anything else to worry about.

"Your grandfather thinks it's okay for you to bring home a bronc?" Her mother was starting to sound just like him.

"Granddad wasn't with me at the cattle auction," Jamie admitted.

"Do I have this right? You bought a horse at the cattle auction, on your own, that you can't even approach . . . Please put Dad on the phone."

"He's asleep," Jamie said. "I can hear him snoring, Mom." Which wasn't exactly true because her grandfather's door was shut, but he probably was sleeping.

"Then I'll call him back tomorrow. Good night, Jamie," her mother said firmly.

She hung up before Jamie could ask her where she was.

Jamie managed to think of one good thing before she fell asleep: *At least I've given Mom and Granddad a reason to speak to each other.*

But she sort of forgot the phone call when she walked into the kitchen early the next morning.

Her granddad was standing near the stove, drinking a cup of coffee.

"How are you doing with Lucky?" he asked as Jamie poured milk into a bowl of Froot Loops. "Think you can get a halter on her in the next few days?"

Jamie set the carton of milk down, suddenly queasy. "Soon. I have almost two months to work with her," she said defensively.

"Will you be able to saddle her and ride her, before you leave here?"

Jamie hadn't thought past getting Lucky used to her, not really. But how long would it be before she'd be able to put her arms around the filly's neck? Weeks?

Which meant it might be a month before she could slip a halter over the filly's head.

Saddling Lucky Lady in the time she'd have left seemed almost impossible. And riding her? No way that was going to happen.

Tears welled up in Jamie's eyes. She bit her bottom lip to keep it from quivering, because her grandfather was studying her face. All at once she was furious with him!

"You knew I couldn't train Lucky on my own! You'll put up with her until I go back to Maine and then send her straight to the auction, right?"

No wonder her mom didn't want to have anything to do with him—he was the meanest man on earth!

"So why don't you get rid of her right now!" Jamie burst out the kitchen door and ran to the corral.

Lucky Lady and Samson were nibbling at a bale of hay without a care in the world. They barely glanced at Jamie as she peered at them through the fence.

Jamie knew her heart would break every time she looked at the filly. She hadn't helped Lucky at all—so she might as well go home. Since her grandfather owed her for all the painting she'd done, she'd ask for the money and fly back to Maine.

Jamie was leaning against the fence, watching Lucky through her tears, when her grandfather walked past her carrying a saddle blanket, a bridle, and his saddle. A coiled rope was hooked to the saddle horn.

Was he actually going to rope the filly while Jamie was standing there? He'd probably called someone to pick her up and haul her away!

But as he opened the east gate into the corral, he said, "If you want to keep this animal we'd better not waste any more time."

"You mean you're not . . . " Jamie was too shocked to finish. She wouldn't have been any more surprised if he'd announced he was moving to Maine himself.

"I said I didn't want a bronc on the place. So we'll have to see to it that she doesn't stay a bronc long."

The horses were almost as startled as Jamie when he stepped into the corral with his saddle. Lucky Lady raced away from him, to linger at the sunny end of the pen, but Samson trotted right up to Jamie's grandfather.

He rubbed the old sorrel's neck. Then he worked the bit into Samson's mouth. The horse lowered his head so that Jamie's granddad could slide the headstall over his ears.

He arranged the saddle blanket on Samson's back. The saddle followed, and he tightened the girth. He flipped the bridle reins over Samson's head and swung himself into the saddle.

When she saw her grandfather sitting on his horse again, Jamie got a lump in her throat—it looked so *right*. But was he really thinking he'd ride Lucky? The filly was young and strong. And wild. And he was seventy-three. What if she threw him off? He could get hurt.

She could kill him! Jamie realized she was much more nervous for him than she was for her horse.

Her grandfather was whistling tunelessly, just the way he used to, while he shook out his rope and re-coiled it.

He hooked the end of the rope to his saddle horn. He pointed Samson's head straight at Lucky, still poised at the sunny end of the corral, and they walked forward purposefully.

Lucky bolted long before they were within roping range, racing back to her spot under the mesquite tree. But Jamie's granddad didn't chase her. Instead, he walked Samson to the fence at the opposite end of the corral.

From the saddle, he pushed open a narrow gate into one of the smaller pens. Then he turned Samson around.

Samson's pace never varied as he carried Mr. Cameron back across the pen, forcing Lucky to run to the sunny end once more.

Jamie's granddad followed her, nudging Samson into an easy gallop. He stopped the sorrel halfway down the pen, but that was too close for Lucky to feel safe. She thought she could stampede right past them to the shady mesquite.

Old Samson was studying her intently, however, and he moved when she did. He turned the buckskin filly back as easily as he'd turned cattle when he was younger.

Lucky retreated to the sunny end again, and took a long, hard look at Samson, hoping to figure out how to get around him.

But Samson was reading her, too. Each time Lucky took a step to one side or the other, Samson took a matching step to block her.

So Lucky examined the fence for an escape route that didn't involve dodging around Samson and Jamie's granddad.

She finally noticed the narrow gate, opened into the smaller pen. She glanced back at Samson. Jamie could almost hear her considering the best move to make.

Jamie's granddad nudged his horse forward a few steps.

That's all it took to push Lucky through the gate, into the small pen beyond it.

Mr. Cameron and Samson walked through the gate, too. Jamie's granddad closed it and latched it behind them.

10

BY THE TIME JAMIE HAD JOGGED ALONG THE corral fence to see what was happening, her grandfather and Samson were standing in the middle of the small pen. Lucky Lady was circling them, hugging the fence, while Mr. Cameron encouraged her to move faster by swinging a length of the coiled rope over his head.

The buckskin filly ran in a circle to the left for a few minutes. Then Jamie's granddad nudged Samson forward a step or two, forcing Lucky to spin around and circle to the right.

Left . . . right . . . left . . . right, without slowing down. Before long, Lucky's neck and shoulders were lathered with sweat.

"Won't she get totally worn out?" Jamie called to her grandfather.

"I'm hoping she will. She's too full of herself for me to feel comfortable with her yet."

Lucky circled and circled. Finally she stopped on her own, and turned toward Mr. Cameron and Samson. She was breathing heavily; her eyes were opened wide. She shifted her feet uncertainly.

Jamie's granddad formed a giant loop in the rope he was holding. He made one swing and lobbed the loop at the filly. It sailed through the air, opening up to drop around Lucky's neck.

She snorted and shied away, but not before Mr. Cameron had ridden forward and dallied the slack in the rope to his saddle horn. The noose tightened around the filly's neck, and she discovered that she was tied fast to Samson, with only ten or twelve feet of rope between them.

Lucky Lady faced Mr. Cameron bravely, determined to fight for her freedom.

But before she could rear up or charge him, he reined Samson in a tight circle toward her right hip.

Lucky had to swing her hindquarters around to keep Samson from bumping into her. The sorrel horse continued to circle, so she had to move her front legs, too, in order to stay balanced.

Hindquarters, front legs, hindquarters, front legs, more times than Jamie could count, until the buckskin filly was moving more freely, almost anticipating the pattern she'd be making as Samson circled her.

That's when Jamie's granddad stopped the sorrel horse, which meant that Lucky could stop, too. The two horses stood still—Samson relaxed, Lucky wary.

Mr. Cameron lifted the rope high in the air so he could rein Samson under it and circle toward Lucky's left side.

"Once I free up her hindquarters," he explained to Jamie, "kind of loosen her up, she'll be less likely to buck with me."

He worked with Lucky from the saddle for an hour or more, patiently but steadily—circling her to the right, then left again, right, left, while the sun climbed higher in the sky.

Then he stopped Samson. When Lucky faced them this time, her head drooped a little.

"Jamie, bring a halter from the barn," Mr. Cameron called out. "And your mother's saddle and a blanket. Come back through the corral."

Jamie jumped down from the fence and ran toward the barn, her stomach doing flip-flops. He was actually going to ride Lucky! Was the filly ready? Was her granddad?

She found a striped saddle blanket and a halter with an eight-foot-long rope hooked to it. Jamie draped the halter over her own head. She dragged the blanket and her mom's saddle out of the barn and across the corral.

Jamie's grandfather had dismounted. He was waiting for her at the narrow gate, while the two horses stood close together in the middle of the small pen. Lucky's rope was still wrapped around Samson's saddle horn, but it hung loosely between them. The old sorrel nuzzled her ear sympathetically.

As Mr. Cameron crossed the pen with the halter, Lucky's head went up, and she stiffened. But she didn't shy away, not even when he reached out to rub her neck. Was she just too tired to move?

Jamie could see Lucky's skin tremble under his hand. But the filly let Jamie's grandfather slide the halter onto her head and reach around her neck to fasten it—she was haltered!

It seemed so easy. But it would have taken Jamie weeks to get to this point.

"There's always one horse in a herd who's in charge, and she knows that's me now," Mr. Cameron was saying as he took the rope from around her neck.

Instead of being Lucky's human boss, Jamie's granddad was thinking like a horse.

Holding the halter rope in his right hand, he repeated the circling on foot, walking toward Lucky's right side, and then her left.

Once the filly was moving easily, he led her closer to the gate and picked up the saddle blanket.

He rubbed the blanket across Lucky's ribs, along her back, and under her belly, as Arnoldo's granddad had described. He even draped it over her tail. The filly twitched every time Mr. Cameron touched her, but she didn't pull away.

Finally he smoothed the blanket out on her back. "They probably got at least this far with her at the Anderson Ranch. And then something went wrong."

"Spurs?" Jamie said, thinking of the gash on Lucky's side.

"Possibly—some horses won't put up with them." Her granddad lifted the saddle and eased it onto the blanket. When Lucky skittered sideways, he circled her again. "If your horse gets scared and acts silly, give her something else to do."

He wasn't just working with Lucky—he was teaching Jamie stuff that he'd spent his whole life learning.

He straightened the filly out until she was standing comfortably again. "Always make sure the cinch is lying flat on the off side," he said, checking the saddle on the right.

He walked back to the filly's left side and reached carefully under her belly for the girth buckle. He threaded the leather strap on the near side of the saddle through the buckle and tightened it. He jiggled the saddle to make sure it was firmly attached to the horse.

Now Jamie crossed her fingers . . . but instead of stepping up into the saddle, her granddad pulled the halter off Lucky's head and waved the filly away from him. He climbed onto Samson and made Lucky circle the pen again—to the left, the right, left, right.

When she finally stopped and turned toward him on her

own, he dismounted and haltered her. He stretched the halter rope back to the saddle horn on Lucky's left side.

Jamie stopped breathing altogether while her granddad took hold of the halter rope and saddle horn. He stuck his foot in the stirrup and pulled himself up slowly . . .

Instead of throwing his right leg over Lucky's back, though, he paused with both of his legs on the filly's left side.

She sidestepped under his weight, but Mr. Cameron pulled on the halter rope, curving the filly's neck to the left. He forced Lucky to circle tightly toward him, so she couldn't buck even if she wanted to.

"I'm letting her get the feel of me," he explained while he leaned across Lucky's back. "If she acts up, I can step off without getting hurt."

Satisfied, he swung his right leg over the saddle, stuck his right foot in the stirrup, and lowered himself into the seat. He loosened his hold on the halter rope and let Lucky straighten out.

Jamie prepared herself for the worst, maybe a stomach-turning, leg-breaking bronc ride. But nothing happened, nothing at all. Her grandfather sat there on her horse for a couple of minutes while Lucky's ears were the only things that moved, swiveling backward and forward.

Then he nudged the filly with his knees, and she walked carefully around the edge of the pen.

After four or five circles, Lucky grew a little more accustomed to having this human on her back. Her muscles eased, and her ears pointed ahead as she focused on where she was going, instead of on what was sitting on top of her.

That's when Jamie's granddad stopped her by pulling back on the halter rope. In a single motion, he slid his foot out of the right stirrup, swung his leg over the saddle, and stepped down to the ground.

"Ready?" he said to Jamie.

"Me?" She'd figured it would be weeks before *she'd* be riding Lucky.

"Come on," said her grandfather.

Her legs felt like lead as she walked through the gate into the smaller pen.

The filly's skin was steaming. She quivered when Jamie reached out to touch her shoulder.

"I've got the halter rope," Jamie's grandfather said. "You just climb on. If she tenses up, I'll handle her."

Jamie barely heard him. When she clutched the saddle horn with both hands and tried to stick her left toe in the stirrup, Lucky danced away from her.

Jamie's grandfather circled the filly several times. "Try again."

She grabbed the saddle horn, gave a little hop, and pulled herself up.

She held her body steady on Lucky's left side for a minute,

as her grandfather had done. Then she swung her right leg over the filly's back and lowered herself slowly into the saddle.

She was sitting on *her* horse, looking down at Lucky's broad, creamy-yellow shoulders, watching the muscles just under the skin twitch a fly away. The filly's ears turned toward her. There was a fine black line around their edges and tiny black tufts at the tips.

As soon as Lucky pricked her ears forward again, Jamie's granddad said, "Let's walk some."

He handed Jamie the end of the halter rope, but his fingers continued to rest on it just below the nosepiece.

He circled the filly to the right for a while, and then to the left. "How does she feel under you? Is she moving freely? Or are her muscles bunched up?"

"She feels . . . okay," Jamie said, afraid to shift even a centimeter in the saddle.

"When I turn loose of the halter rope, you take up the slack. Ready?"

Jamie grabbed the rope lower down, and he let go. As Lucky watched him walk away from them, Jamie gripped the saddle horn so tightly with her left hand that her fingers ached. Would the filly buck?

Lucky didn't budge.

"Nudge her."

Jamie pressed her knees against the stirrup leathers, and

gasped when the filly scooted forward. As soon as she stopped pressing, though, Lucky slowed down to a walk.

"Let her go where she wants."

The filly walked straight into a corner of the pen and stood there with her head lowered.

"Nudge her on the left."

When Jamie squeezed her left leg against the filly's side, Lucky headed down the fence.

After they'd circled the pen a couple of times, Mr. Cameron called out, "Turn Lucky toward me."

Jamie maneuvered with the halter rope until the filly walked to the center of the pen where he was standing. Lucky's head bobbed loosely with each step she took—she looked all worn out.

Mr. Cameron took hold of the halter rope so that Jamie could dismount.

"Thank you, Granddad—that was amazing!" Jamie exclaimed after she'd climbed down. "And I'm . . . sorry for what I said before."

"You weren't so far off. I guess I *was* counting on you to give up on this filly. But you fooled me. And I'm proud of you." He smiled at her.

Jamie reached out to stroke Lucky's face.

She'd never give up on Lucky, not now.

11

AMIE AND HER GRANDFATHER DROVE INTO Wilcox for more paint to finish her mom's room. She worked on the walls in there until early evening.

She didn't realize her mother hadn't called until she was getting ready for bed.

"She's busy traveling around in the wilderness," Jamie told herself while she brushed her teeth. She imagined her mom in a little motorboat, chugging up a wide river lined with houses on stilts.

She slept on the couch that night, too, but the phone didn't ring.

The next morning, Jamie and her granddad set to work with Lucky early, while it was still cool outside.

Mr. Cameron repeated everything he'd done the day before, circling the filly around the pen with Samson, then on foot with the halter without a saddle, and again after he'd saddled her.

He turned her loose in the pen with the saddle on her back, to get all the kinks out. She galloped along the fence, stirrups flopping against her sides.

After a couple of circles, Lucky slowed down, turned, and walked right up to Jamie and her granddad. It really was like *magic*.

The day before, no one could have gotten close to Lucky for longer than a couple of seconds. Touching her would have been a struggle. But twenty-four hours later, the buckskin filly waited quietly for Mr. Cameron to slide the halter over her head.

"Not magic—just horse sense and a little patience," he said, as though he'd guessed what Jamie was thinking.

"So why doesn't everybody train horses this way? Without tying up their legs or using whips or spurs or riding them until they're broken?" Jamie asked.

"They don't want to take the time. Or they just don't have the same horse information that I have after sixty or so years," he replied, placing the saddle on Lucky's back and buckling the girth. "I've been doing this since I was younger than you."

Lucky's ears were pricked forward, her eyes watchful, but she stood quietly while he stretched the halter rope back to the saddle horn.

"Ready to ride?"

"Uh-huh." Jamie pulled herself up on Lucky and into the saddle, as smoothly as if she'd been riding the filly for years. She pressed Lucky's sides with her knees, and they trotted down the fence.

Jamie worked with Lucky for an hour or so, until she could rein the filly to both sides with the halter rope.

"Good," her grandfather said. "Let's jerk the saddle off, lead her over to the house, and give her a bath."

Lucky Lady had never seen water streaming out of a hose before. Jamie sprayed her sweaty back, raising tiny puffs of steam, and she danced around at the end of the halter rope. But soon she began to enjoy her shower. Lucky got a sleepy look in her eyes, and she lowered her head so that Jamie could wash under her mane.

"I believe she's taking to it," Jamie's grandfather said.

"She really *loves* it!"

When Lucky shook herself like a dog, flinging water all over Jamie, her grandfather laughed. "She's telling you she's had enough."

A few swipes with a rubber currycomb, and Lucky's coat

was slick and clean, her mane hung neatly on the left side of her neck, and even her hoofs gleamed. Jamie thought the filly looked as pretty as any show horse.

That afternoon, Jamie cooled herself off in the Ochoas' pool. She and Arnoldo swam for a couple of hours, and Mr. Ochoa grilled hamburgers for an early dinner.

The whole Ochoa family and Jamie were eating at the wooden table on the patio when Arnoldo's mom asked, "Where's your mother this week, Jamie?"

"Vietnam."

"Vietnam?" She and her husband glanced at each other.

"Why?" Was something wrong?

"Um . . . did you watch the news last night?" said Mr. Ochoa.

Jamie shook her head, really worried now.

"Vietnam was hit by a huge tropical storm yesterday," Mrs. Ochoa said. "The whole bottom half of the country is flooded."

Was that why Jamie hadn't heard from her mom? Suddenly, she needed to be with her granddad more than anything.

"Would you mind taking me home?"

"No problem at all." Mr. Ochoa pushed his plate back and jumped to his feet.

◆   ◆   ◆

Jamie and her grandfather watched the six o'clock news, sitting close together on the living-room couch.

"The typhoon season started early this year. A huge storm struck the Mekong Delta in Vietnam late yesterday," the newscaster said. "Winds were clocked at over one hundred ten, and were accompanied by torrential rains. Rivers and canals rose as much as four feet an hour."

Jamie's grandfather slipped his arm around her shoulders.

There was footage of houses reduced to tumbled piles of wood scraps and tin. People and animals huddled on rooftops while the floodwaters rose.

"The death toll is at four hundred twenty and climbing," the newscaster went on, "with hundreds more missing. The damage to crops and property is in the millions."

Mr. Cameron switched off the television. "I'll bet this storm wasn't as bad as they're making it sound, Jamie."

Later that evening, however, it sounded even worse. Rivers were cresting at thirty feet above flood stage in places. Jamie remembered the image she'd had of her mother, exploring the delta in a small boat. Where was she now?

"Carolyn's gonna call," Jamie's grandfather said. "I'm sure of it."

But she didn't call that night or the next day, either.

Jamie and her granddad worked with Lucky Lady the next two mornings, even though their hearts weren't really in it—but the filly tried hard to please.

To keep busy in the afternoons, Jamie started painting her grandfather's bedroom a bright green.

She couldn't really eat, she couldn't sleep without having nightmares about giant storms, and she could hardly think about anything but her mom. Was she stranded somewhere?

Or worse. Could she be . . . dead? Jamie had already lost one parent. She couldn't imagine life without her mother.

The morning of the third day, Mr. Cameron decided to drive into Wilcox. "I'll talk to Sylvia Soliz at the courthouse—maybe she can find out something for us on her computer. Want to come?"

Jamie shook her head. "I'll stay here, in case we get a call."

She was sitting in the living room, staring at the telephone and trying to will it to ring, when there was a knock at the kitchen door.

She raced into the kitchen, hoping someone had good news for her.

It was Arnoldo.

"Oh. Hi," Jamie said listlessly.

"Want to go bike riding?"

"Uh-uh, I have to . . . "

All at once she just had to get out of the house. "Let's take the horses for a walk."

"Can't they walk themselves?" Arnoldo said.

"No, we'll lead them over to the pond in the next pasture.

They can take a bath—Lucky loves water—and we can wade around."

Arnoldo shrugged. "Okay."

He was wearing shorts. Jamie put on her bathing suit under her jeans and switched her boots for sneakers.

She wrote a quick note to her granddad—*With Arnoldo at the stock tank*—and stuck it in the screen door as they left the house.

12

$\mathcal{L}$UCKY LADY AND SAMSON WERE STANDING IN THE corral, sleepily swatting at flies. But they perked up as soon as Jamie and Arnoldo stepped through the gate.

When the filly lowered her head to let Jamie slide a halter over her ears, Arnoldo exlaimed, "Last week we couldn't have gotten in the same pen with her—excellent job!"

Jamie helped him halter Samson, and they led the two horses to the dirt road, turning toward the next pasture.

"How far are we going?" Arnoldo pushed his dark glasses

onto the top of his head. "It's so hot my shades are fogging up."

"The stock tank's not more than a mile and a half away."

Jamie and Lucky plodded along behind Arnoldo and Samson, the filly not really paying attention to where she was going until they reached the next pasture. Then she spotted some of Mr. Yates's cows resting in the shade of a mesquite.

Lucky stopped short and raised her head to sniff the air.

"What's the matter with her?" Arnoldo said over his shoulder. "It's not like she hasn't seen cows before."

"I think she's figuring out what they're likely to do, where they might run." Lucky would probably make a good cow horse, maybe even better than Samson. She might do well at quarter horse shows, too, penning cattle.

Which made Jamie think of her mom again.

Mom's okay, she told herself sternly. *Of course she's okay.*

Jamie tugged on the halter rope to get Lucky's attention. "Come on, before I fry out here." She could feel the tip of her nose starting to sunburn.

They crossed the open prairie and wound their way through the mesquite thicket that surrounded the windmill, until they arrived at the open space near the tower.

"So where's the pond? I'm ready to melt," Arnoldo said.

"Right over that dirt dam," Jamie told him.

Then Lucky must have smelled the water, because she bounded up the mound of earth so fast that Jamie had to scramble to keep up with her. The filly trotted straight into the pond, until the water lapped against her belly. Jamie's clothes were soaked and her sneakers were probably wrecked, but the cool water made her feel more cheerful.

Lucky bent her front legs and collapsed into the pond. She sent a wave toward the bank that startled dozens of frogs. They dove into the water, reappearing to bob on the surface near Arnoldo.

He'd sat down closer to the bank, the water up to his chin. And Samson's head was half submerged—he was prospecting for pond weeds.

"This is great!" Arnoldo shouted happily.

"The best." Red and green dragonflies wheeled over Jamie's head, and doves cooed in the mesquite trees beyond the tower. For the moment, at least, she had the feeling that everything might turn out all right.

"I hear a car engine. Think your granddad's coming?" Arnoldo asked a little uneasily.

Jamie heard it, too, the distant sputtering of a motor. But the sounds didn't seem to be growing any louder, and she shook her head.

Lucky clambered to her feet and blew her nose enthusiastically.

Jamie rubbed the filly's wet neck. Then she placed her left hand on Lucky's withers, and her right hand on her rump. She hadn't ever ridden Lucky without her granddad close by, and never bareback. But in three-and-a-half feet of water, there wasn't much of a risk . . .

She draped the halter rope across the filly's neck, stood on tiptoe, and boosted herself out of the water, until she was lying across Lucky's back. When she reached for the filly's mane to steady herself, though, Lucky quickly sidestepped. Jamie slid off her back into the pond.

Lucky curved her neck around to stare at Jamie with such a quizzical expression that both she and Arnoldo burst out laughing.

They hung out in the water with the horses until their fingers started to wrinkle. Then they sat on the bank and dried off in the sun while Lucky and Samson nibbled at dry grass.

Jamie and Arnoldo were tossing sticks into the pond for the frogs to use as rafts when a sharp smell drifted in on the breeze, tickling Jamie's nose.

"Is that smoke?" she said, sitting up straighter.

Arnoldo sniffed. "I don't smell anything. Or see anything either," he added, gazing at the clear blue sky over their heads.

But only a couple of minutes had passed when he changed his mind. "I smell it now." He stood up fast.

"Could it be a brush fire?" Jamie said, standing up, too.

"Let's check it out—remember that car we heard? It could have sparked something."

They led the horses around the windmill and through the mesquites.

Arnoldo and Samson reached the edge of the trees first.

"Bummer!" Arnoldo muttered.

Jamie stepped up beside him and saw it herself, a long line of flickering flames and dark smoke on the far side of the dirt road. And her heart felt as though it might pound through her chest.

Lucky was staring at the fire, too. She fidgeted nervously, tugging at the halter rope.

Arnoldo wet his index finger in his mouth and held it up in the air. "The wind's blowing the fire toward the west. If we go east, we can make it through the gate and over to the ranch house. Or to the highway if we need to—brush fires usually won't jump a wide strip of pavement."

The words were hardly out of his mouth when the wind shifted, and so did the fire.

"Now it's coming this way, Arnoldo!" Jamie said softly, as if she were afraid the flames might hear her.

"We better get out of here!" He jogged away from the windmill with Samson at his heels—the old sorrel horse was just as eager to put some distance between himself and the fire as Arnoldo was.

But Lucky seemed hypnotized by the blaze. She planted her feet and watched as two white-tailed deer raced out of the smoke.

"Come on, girl," Jamie coaxed, putting all her weight on the halter rope.

Not until Samson whinnied urgently did Lucky come out of her trance. She whinnied a reply and trotted quickly after the sorrel horse, Jamie sprinting alongside her. They hadn't gone far when, in a split second, Jamie's left foot dropped straight down about fifteen inches; she'd stepped into a gopher hole.

She pitched forward and felt a stabbing pain in her lower leg. Jamie caught herself before she fell flat on the ground, but she lost her grip on Lucky's halter rope. When she looked up, her horse was galloping toward Arnoldo and Samson.

"Arnoldo—grab Lucky!" she screamed.

He snagged the end of the halter rope as the buckskin filly circled them. "Got her! What happened?"

Jamie was working her foot out of the gopher hole. Her left ankle was already beginning to swell, and it throbbed with every heartbeat. The fire was burning closer—now she could hear the crackling of the flames.

"Are you hurt?" Arnoldo called to her.

Jamie shook her head and forced herself to her feet.

When she tried to hobble forward, though, he yelled, "Stay where you are!" He turned the two horses around and led them quickly back to Jamie.

She was balancing on her right foot. "It's my ankle."

"Is it broken?" His eyes slid toward the approaching fire, and back to Jamie.

"A bad sprain, I think—I can't step on it."

The blaze was scattering Mr. Yates's cattle. Lucky's ears swiveled toward them as they ran scared across the pasture.

"I'll turn the horses loose and help you," Arnoldo said, reaching for the buckle of Samson's halter.

Jamie grabbed Lucky's halter rope away from him. "No! We can't turn them loose—they might die! We can ride them. . . ." That is if the filly trusted her enough to let her climb on, bareback, in the middle of nowhere, with a brush fire sweeping toward them.

"I'm not a cowboy, and I'm not riding anybody. *We'll* die if we don't clear out of here," Arnoldo said grimly.

But Jamie was determined to save her horse. "I'm riding Lucky—I can't walk. And Samson will follow us, so you can run along with him. If you'll give me a boost . . ."

Arnoldo didn't waste any more time arguing—he dropped to one knee. "Stand on my leg."

Jamie pulled the filly closer to Arnoldo. "Please, Lucky, be cool," she murmured, holding onto the halter rope and clutching the filly's black mane with both hands.

She stepped up onto Arnoldo's leg, ignoring the searing pain in her left ankle. She flung herself across Lucky's back before the filly could dance too far away from her.

Jamie's head and shoulders were on one side of the horse, her legs on the other.

She felt Lucky's muscles knotting up under her stomach. The horse's ears were pinned back . . .

She's going to throw me off, and then the fire'll catch me! A big mesquite burst into a ball of flame, and Lucky stamped her front feet nervously. Jamie wriggled sideways far enough to wrap her arms around Lucky's neck. Then she swung her right leg over the filly's rump.

She sat up on Lucky's back and pulled on the halter rope. As she walked the filly in a circle she could see that the fire had curved halfway around them already.

"We can't make it to the gate," she told Arnoldo, trying to keep the panic out of her voice. Where could they go?

Lucky gave her the answer. When the filly straightened out, she strained at her halter, eager to race back to the windmill.

"Arnoldo, we might be safe in the pond," Jamie said urgently. "Can you . . . "

"Don't worry about me—just go!"

Jamie let Lucky have her head. The filly broke into a smooth gallop, and Jamie silently thanked her grandfather for everything he'd taught her.

"And thank you, too, Lucky," she said as she clung to the filly's mane.

Arnoldo and Samson ran after them, the fire not far behind.

13

THE GROUP CHARGED THROUGH THE MESQUITE thicket, Jamie ducking low over Lucky's neck so she wouldn't get swept off by low-hanging limbs. They dodged around the windmill tower and bounded over the dirt dam to wade out into the center of the pond. Jamie slid off the filly into water up to her chest. Arnoldo and Samson splashed up next to them.

Gripping the halter ropes, Jamie and Arnoldo patted the horses and talked to them reassuringly, while the air around them grew dark with dense gray smoke and as hot as an oven.

"The mesquite thicket's catching!" Arnoldo said, starting to cough. Jamie felt the acrid fumes all the way down in her lungs.

Flames flickered in the tops of the trees that ringed the stock tank. There was a loud *crack*—a large branch exploded in the blaze—and both horses shied in the water.

Lucky snorted loudly and jerked at the halter rope. Samson stared skyward at burning embers floating toward the pond.

"Sparks. Get your hair wet." Arnoldo ducked his head under the water.

Jamie dunked hers, too. "What about the horses? Take off your T-shirt, Arnoldo—I'll hold Samson."

After Arnoldo had peeled his shirt off, she pulled her own T-shirt over her head, stripping down to her bathing suit.

They soaked the T-shirts in the pond and wrung them out over the horses' necks and backs. Then they draped the wet shirts over Lucky and Samson's ears.

Suddenly two red cows and a calf stampeded over the dirt dam and splashed into the pond, so close to them that Jamie could smell the animals' singed hair.

A mesquite right next to the water ignited and burned merrily. The cattle edged even closer to the kids and the horses. They moaned low in their throats.

Arnoldo was choking. Jamie pulled the wet T-shirt off Lucky's head and handed it to him, saying, "Breathe through this."

The filly lowered her head so that her face rested against Jamie's body as the brush fire jumped to a clump of thorny bushes and then to a large stand of prickly pear and melted it like rubber.

Even the horses were coughing now. The heat was intense. All at once, the cows stampeded again, splashing out of the water to dash into the burning trees. The little calf bawled for his mother, but he was too small to move quickly across the pond. Before he'd made it halfway to the bank, Lucky blocked him, pushing him into deeper water again.

A few seconds later, Jamie and Arnoldo heard blood-curdling bellows from the cows—the fire had caught them.

"Lucky saved that calf's life," Arnoldo croaked.

His face was smudged with soot and his eyes were bright red and streaming from the smoke. It was so thick that Jamie couldn't see the windmill tower.

Arnoldo wheezed with every breath. Jamie was having trouble breathing herself. And she was losing heart.

If we don't burn we'll suffocate. She'd never find out if her mom was okay. She thought about her granddad, too: *He won't ever get over this.*

She hoped dying wouldn't hurt too much and that she'd be brave. That's when Arnoldo reached out and took her hand. He squeezed it, she squeezed back, but neither of them said anything.

Lucky pressed against Jamie's right side. She closed her

eyes, imagining her mother standing outside their house in Maine in the snow. Taking shallow, gasping breaths, she waited for it all to be over . . .

Suddenly Arnoldo said, "Jamie!"

She opened her eyes. The wind was picking up, and it seemed to be blowing the fire back into the trees that were already ablaze. She struggled to speak: "Is it turning around?"

"Yeah, it could burn itself out!"

They waited in the pond for what seemed like an hour, until the blackened brush around them barely smoldered, and the air had cooled a little.

The horses were quiet. The calf had edged closer and closer to Lucky until it was leaning against her front leg, its nose barely clearing the water.

At last, Arnoldo grinned at Jamie. "I think we made it!" he said, and coughed so hard that Samson turned his head to stare at him.

"We made it!" Jamie repeated in disbelief. She hugged the filly's neck and whispered, "You *are* lucky!"

Then they heard a car honking not far away.

"That sounds like my dad's Jeep—come on, Jamie!" Arnoldo was ready to wade out of the pond with Samson.

"Leave him with me—you go. I can't walk on this ankle, anyway," Jamie told him. "Plus I've got the calf."

Arnoldo splashed slowly through the water, still coughing, and walked into the blackened trees at the far end of the pond.

Jamie was still standing waist deep in water with all the animals around her, glad to be alive, when someone shouted, "Jamie?"

"I'm here, Granddad!"

Her grandfather clambered over the dam and jumped into the water with his boots on. He hugged Jamie so hard that he lifted her right out of the pond. "Arnoldo told me about your ankle. Are you all right otherwise?"

"Uh-huh," she said, her grimy face mashed against his white Western shirt.

"I can't believe you made it through this!" he murmured, looking at the charred trunks of the mesquites ringing the stock tank.

A thin layer of soot covered the ground as far as they could see.

Jamie's granddad carried her out of the pond and set her down on the bank. Samson and Lucky followed, with the calf at Lucky's heels. They were gathered on the dam when Uncle Tomas stepped out of the scorched trees. He was wearing a yellow rubber coat with WILCOX VOLUNTEER FIRE DEPARTMENT printed on the sleeve, and black rubber boots.

"Am I glad to see you in one piece!" He hugged Jamie. "And this buckskin filly, too."

"But where's Arnoldo?" Jamie asked him.

"Lying down in the Jeep—he got kind of dizzy from breathing the smoke. But his dad's taking care of him, and he'll be fine," Uncle Tomas said. "All of you will," he added, rubbing old Samson's head. "Ready, Mr. Cameron? If you carry Jamie, I'll lead these horses, and the baby calf'll come, along . . ."

Tomas grabbed the halter ropes and headed into the trees with Lucky and Samson. The calf stayed close to Lucky's hindquarters—he'd adopted the filly as his mother.

Jamie's granddad started after them with Jamie in his arms. "When I saw the fire, and then I read your note . . . " He cleared his throat and didn't finish.

Jamie looked up at him and thought his blue eyes looked a little damp. "I'm okay, Granddad—really," she said.

The grass beyond the mesquite thicket had been reduced to a powdery ash. Not too far away, Jamie picked out two charred lumps that might have been the cows.

That could have been us. Despite the heat she shivered.

Arnoldo was sitting in the passenger seat of the Ochoas' Jeep with his head back. His dad was standing beside him, looking concerned.

But Arnoldo sat up when he heard them coming toward him. "Dad said every fire truck in the county was lined up on the highway, Jamie!" he exclaimed. "This was major!"

Then he coughed like his lungs might shatter.

"Arnoldo, don't talk until you're breathing a little better!" Mr. Ochoa told him. "Jamie looks like she's had enough excitement, anyway." He smiled at her. "Thank goodness you're here—both of you."

Uncle Tomas had picked up the baby calf. "What should we do with this guy?"

"Wait until I put Jamie down." Her granddad placed her carefully in the back of the Jeep. When Tomas deposited the baby calf next to her, he lay his head on Jamie's knee and fell immediately asleep.

As her grandfather squeezed into the Jeep beside them, Jamie asked quietly, "Did the ranch house burn, Granddad?"

"No—the fire did cross the fence between this pasture and the house, but then it doubled back." He put his hand on Jamie's shoulder, as if to reassure himself that she was safe. "We'd better get you home and take care of that ankle."

"Not without Lucky." Jamie and Arnoldo had gotten the horses safely through a brush fire—she wasn't going to leave her filly behind now. "And Samson."

Tomas and Mr. Ochoa were holding onto the horses' halter ropes.

"I'll lead Samson from back here, and Lucky will follow along," Mr. Cameron said.

"What about you, Tío?" Arnoldo asked, because they'd run out of space in the Jeep.

"There's a stump-jumper on the other side of the windmill," he said. "I'll catch a ride on it."

"Can we take a look, Dad?" Arnoldo said excitedly, and broke into a coughing fit.

"No way—you're going home!" said his father.

"Catch you later, bro," Tomas said to him. "See you soon, Jamie."

He walked back toward the windmill, and Jamie and her granddad and the other Ochoas bounced across the pasture in the Jeep, headed for the ranch house. Samson trotted alongside, with Lucky just a couple of strides behind him.

While Jamie's granddad got her settled on the living room couch, Mr. Ochoa carried the calf into the backyard. "I'd better get Arnoldo into town to show him to his mother," he said from the kitchen door. "She'll want to count every hair on his head to make sure he's okay."

Jamie could hear Arnoldo still coughing.

"Maybe we'll run him past the health clinic," his dad added.

"Might be a good idea," said Jamie's grandfather.

He called Dr. Garza in Wilcox, who drove out to the ranch to take a look at Jamie's ankle.

"It's not broken or fractured—it's just a bad sprain," the doctor said after he'd examined it. "But you'll have to stay off that foot for a week or so and keep it taped."

It wasn't until he left that Jamie asked her grandfather if he had any news about her mom.

"Sylvia at the courthouse got in touch with the State Department on her computer," he said. "But it may be several days before we hear anything."

Jamie tried to fight back tears, but she couldn't—she put her head on her arms and sobbed.

Her granddad sat down on the couch next to her. "I've asked myself for the last few years why your mother wouldn't live right here at the ranch with you, where I could keep an eye on you both. But I guess we have to let people live their own lives, even if we love them."

"Especially if we love them," Jamie agreed, wiping her eyes.

14

$\mathscr{J}$AMIE COULDN'T MAKE HERSELF LIE AROUND THE house past breakfast the next morning. She wanted to see how Lucky was doing, so she hopped out to the corral on her good foot to watch her granddad ride.

"We don't want her to forget anything she's learned," he said as he saddled the filly. "And if she studies cows like you think she does . . . we might start training her to pen cattle before long."

Mr. Cameron was loping Lucky in easy circles along the

corral fence, warming her up, when Jamie thought she heard a faint ringing.

She raced toward the house without giving her ankle a thought, even with her granddad shouting after her, "Jamie, be careful of that foot!"

And it *was* the phone ringing. She threw open the screen door and limped through the kitchen and into the living room to grab it.

"Huh-hello?" She was trying to catch her breath.

The line sounded dead, so she was about to hang up when a faraway voice said, "Hello? Hello? Jamie?"

"Mom!" Jamie shrieked. "Mom! Mom! Is it really you? Where are you? Were you caught in that storm? Are you okay?"

"I'm okay, just a little damp and very hungry," her mother said. "I was stranded on a tiny island with no food or clean water for four days and nights with at least three hundred other people. All I could think about was seeing you and . . ."

Jamie's granddad hustled into the living room and stuck his hand out for the phone.

"Hello. Carolyn?" he said. "Are you all right? . . . Yes, Jamie and I saw it on the news. She was afraid . . . we were afraid you might be caught in the worst of . . . she's doing fine. She keeps me busy."

He went on, "The filly is coming along. . . . Yes, I started her, but Jamie's riding her already. . . . That's right . . . I know how happy she'd be to have you come," he said. "I'd like it, too . . . Of course, Carolyn—any time you can . . ."

He cleared his throat. "All right, call us tomorrow," and he hung up the phone.

"Did she sound okay to you?" Jamie asked him.

"She sounded just like herself," her grandfather answered. "She had to give somebody else a turn at the phone. But she said she'll fly down at the end of the summer to see you ride Lucky Lady."

"I was kind of hoping she'd come now." More than anything, Jamie would like her mom to be standing right there in front of them.

"Well, your mother has a job to finish. I feel like celebrating! What would you like to do? Have lunch in Wilcox, maybe?"

"Uh-uh—watch you ride Lucky."

"I'll be happy to."

But before he went out to the corral again, he dialed Sylvia at the courthouse to let her know about Jamie's mom.

As Jamie hobbled into the kitchen, she was thinking how much things had changed since she'd arrived in Texas. She had her own horse, her grandfather was riding again instead of talking about how old he was, she'd practically sat on a rattlesnake, and had lived through a brush fire. She'd even painted most of the house.

How had all of this happened in less than two weeks?

Jamie pushed open the screen door to look at her filly standing near the corral fence. When Lucky saw her, she raised her head in the air and nickered a greeting.

And Jamie answered her own question: *Just Lucky, I guess.*